YOU

or the Invention
of Memory

YOU

or the Invention
of Memory

a novel

JONATHAN BAUMBACH

DZANC
BOOKS

The characters and events in this book are fictitious. Any similarity to real persons, living or dead, is coincidental and not intended by the author.

Book design by Steven Seighman

ISBN: 978-1-936873-71-5

First edition: November 2012

ART WORKS.
arts.gov

michigan council for
arts and cultural affairs

This project is supported in part by an award from the National Endowment for the Arts and the Michigan Council for Arts and Cultural Affairs.

Printed in the United States of America

10   9   8   7   6   5   4   3   2   1

to you

I remember nothing as it was.
What I remember—all I remember is at it is.

—MIGUEL FUNES (translated by the author)

PART

I

ONE

You are warily approaching the first sentence of my new novel, not wanting to be taken unaware, or not wanting to be plunged into something from which there is no perceptible exit or perhaps both at once, separate and inseparable concerns.

The opening sentence, with your unspoken consent, has edged its way into the barely remembered past.

You are now looking at the third sentence of this still untitled work. I imagine you reading my words as they come to mind so in a certain sense you can say that I am writing them for you, which is only true in the most reductive context. I am writing this novel because writing novels is what I do and my inner clock tells me— this is just a metaphor, you understand, I have no inner clock—that the moment has come to put everything else aside and begin the next chapter in my extended story as novelist. There is no particular reason why I am beginning now and not last month or tomorrow or the week after next. That's just the way it happened to play out.

It was, in fact, this morning, after my breakfast of muesli with fourteen slices of banana and a touch of yogurt, after checking out last night's scores, after taking my 7-minute shower, that the book you are reading announced its intention to get its not quite fully imagined presence on the page.

Let me say, before I get on with the game, why I imagine you as my reader and not someone else. Writing a novel for all its aggressive gyrations, for all its assaultive and invasive aspects, is a gesture of love between writer and reader. In whatever transactions there have been between us over the years, I am aware that you have been the more loving. So this novel, which I'm writing with you in mind as its reader, is a way, as I see it, of redressing that discrepancy. I realize that this is a displaced gesture, but given my emotional limitations it is tantamount to taking off my clothes under a spotlight on a public stage. No appreciation is asked for or expected. But that's not absolutely true. Relying on your generosity, I hope that you will stay with me, even in the face of disappointment, to the final gesture of this book—the last word of the last sentence.

Before I get too far along, I'd first like to get your opinion of the novel's informing idea, which is this. A writer, not me exactly, though someone so much like me that only you could tell us apart, is addressing his not-yet-fully-conceived novel to an unnamed woman, known only as "you," who is, though you might not see it this way at all, a coded version of you. The novel, while not itself a love letter, is offered as an expression of love in that it is written with a sustained vision of you processing each word.

You may find this a larger burden than you want to take on and, if so, I apologize in advance. Still, I've disguised the facts of our not easily definable relationship sufficiently to protect your privacy. Whatever other readers choose to think, no one can know absolutely that the "you" of the novel is you unless you make a point of acknowledging it. You may even have your doubts—fiction, as you know, is its own code—but all I can do is assure you that if it's not you, it's no one else.

So that's the premise of this book, or, if you will, its argument. Where's the universality, you might ask, or someone less generously disposed, a critic perhaps, might ask. Its universality is in its particulars, I am quick to answer, but you are right to think that my reply is evasive. Where are its characters beyond the generic abstractions of you and me? What's the story it wants to tell?

All of these questions will be answered, I want to believe, at some point in the proceedings, or possibly not. The fact is, I don't have a clue right now as to what comes next. The book you are reading— are you still with me?—is making itself up, catch as catch can, as it goes along.

I am hoping to tell a story that, among a universe of stories, would be the one, if you had world enough and time, you would like most to read while reclining in your queen-sized bed, head propped up at a 60 degree angle on a cushion of three goose down pillows. My knowing your favorite authors is of no help, is of negative help, in the present situation. To imitate a book you (and I) admire would be to offer, inescapably, a secondhand pleasure. I also happen to know how much you dislike false sentiment so, insofar as I'm in control of what I'm doing, you'll find no appeals, spurious or otherwise, to the oversubscribed heart.

Of course placing all these restrictions on my narrative makes it a little tricky to get the ship out of port.

What I may have to do, assuming a certain sympathy between us, is write the book necessity and obsession dictate and trust that you will find its story at once familiar and strange. It will be a test case for both of us in that if the book means nothing to you neither of us is the person the other imagined.

Of course if you don't respond to the book, if you don't love it so to speak, it may only be that I have failed to realize my vision.

I am considering telling two stories, on the surface quite different from one another, spliced together in alternating sentences. Not alternating sentences perhaps—that might give you a headache or cause you to throw the book against the wall, which could cause damage to the spine—but, say alternating paragraphs or alternating pages. I might have to settle for alternating chapters.

For as long as I've known you, you've been an unblushing admirer of the bold and unexpected. The book I am writing with you in mind will be nothing if not unexpected.

I am trying to remember the first time I was aware of your existence. We were at a large party, as I recall, and I noticed you on the other side of the room talking to someone I knew slightly. It struck me that I might go over to this distant acquaintance and say hello and so wangle an introduction, but then you moved on to someone else or someone engaged me in a conversation and I lost sight of you. Eight months passed before I saw you again.

Leaving the party, we rode down together in a crowded elevator, each looking at our shoes. Of course, I can only really speak for my own averted glance but given the sympathy we shared from the outset, I imagine we were both employing the same evasive tactic.

My shoes, as I recall, were New Balance cross trainers with an ostentatious gray and yellow design.

Years later, when we were already friends, I never mentioned to you that I had been aware of you, had kissed your knee, the left I believe (perhaps it was the right) in the imagination's overheated bedroom, long before we were introduced.

It's odd, but I can't remember the occasion when we were actually presented to one another, which only means that our relationship begins and ends for me in the conflation of memory and fantasy, and the literal moment of our meeting is unimportant, just a passing blip in an extensive continuum.

Perhaps we introduced ourselves and this meeting I can't remember took place in another elevator in a different building going up to the penthouse apartment of another party.

"We've met before," I said to you (I believe).

"Have we?" you said, studying my face for clues. "I'm sure I would have remembered."

"Thank you," I said and you looked oddly at me then. What I took to be a compliment, that I was unforgettable in some not easily defined way, had been meant as something else. I think it was what I admired most about you, your capacity to keep those who aspired to get close to you slightly off-balance. You were seeing someone, you let me know, though you accepted my offer to go somewhere for a cup of coffee. That may have been another time, a time I bumped into you at a publication party at an overcrowded West Side apartment, and I've dovetailed the two in memory.

We went for a drink instead of coffee, didn't we, though at that point we were both already sufficiently besotted. The place we chose—it was more that the place chose us—was too noisy for conversation and so we went to my apartment, which was only a few blocks away, to continue our tenuous connection.

Unless my memory is even more unreliable than I suspect, that was the only time we went to bed together. Its awkwardness was what made it so touching and memorable. An intensity of feeling undermined the elegance of the act itself.

You warned me afterward that what happened between us would never be repeated. Never, you insisted, though not without notable regret. Still, I remained hopeful that a time would come eventually, a sudden change of emotional season, and we would again fall into each other's despairing embrace as we had that first night. In the mean time, we became friends—at least that's how it reads in my scenario—better friends no doubt than had we continued as lovers.

I'd like to believe that that's what you had in mind when you announced with that unwavering certainty so characteristic of your style, moments after our artless grappling on my unmade bed, that this was it, the first and last and only time.

There were other opportunities, other evenings when I sensed you were willing, but you see, and I'm sure you knew this all along, I felt as your friend that it would be a form of betrayal to undermine your resolve.

The sexual afterglow I carried around with me for months, years perhaps, after our near-miraculous improvisatory encounter eventually dissipated or metamorphosed, as I like to think, into a kind of extraordinary sympathy that transcended the need for sexual affirmation.

If none of this meets with your view of how things started between us, it may be because I have a history of confusing the real world with the more compelling narrative of my fantasies. My story, I'm embarrassed to admit, is infinitely revisable. And so—you would be the one to make this determination—our history may be just another fantasy in that baroque chimera I have the dishonor to call my life.

I did, as it happens, write a story based on my subjective experience of our relationship with a very different conclusion from the way things between us actually played out. It seems fitting to me that that story should be a part of this novel you are reading and, in time (and space), it will earn its way into these pages. I don't want any surprises. I want it all to surprise.

Before I move on, before I get what needs to be behind us filed away, I want to make one last disclaimer. The things I've said to you here I've also in the past said to others and will, as history repeats itself, say again to others still, which doesn't make them any the less sincere. At least in your case, I never cease to mean them.

Well, isn't that the kind of thing every con man says? I am a liar. I freely confess—no knife at my throat—that I make things up and therefore (with expectation of your acceptance) I'm asking for your trust. If you can't trust me, who has shown you his most disreputable side, who can you trust?

Before we actually met, I said to you in the elevator, muttered it in a way to make it impossible for you to be certain that you heard anything at all—remember we were both looking at our feet at the time—that ... Perhaps you heard me and only pretended not to.

In any event, you didn't respond and I did not repeat my aggressive petition. It is probably a flaw in my nature but I'd rather—perhaps this was not so true when I was younger—be loved than fucked.

So as we became close friends it was a tacit agreement between us that the prospect of sex was outside the equation of our friendship. Whatever sexual feelings came up in our encounters would of necessity be repressed and, for the sake of civility, denied. Sex between us, penis entering vagina (grappling like swans among soiled sheets), prick stabbing cunt, would not be thought about or, if thought about, would not be acknowledged.

Friendship was the be-all and end-all of our relationship.

And you have been a good friend, I'll give you that, a loving friend who asks for virtually nothing in return. If I need a place to stay in an emergency, I know I can count on you to offer me a bed for the night. Not yours, but the one in your study that has a secret identity during the day as a couch. Nor did you mind, or seem to mind, listening to stories of my wife's infidelities.

I should confess that there was only one infidelity and that I elaborated for the sake of a better story. I didn't want to lose your attention. Mostly everything in my life is subordinate to the endlessly variable story that I offer in its place.

TWO

———

An arbitrary last minute decision brings me to a publishing party in a cramped Upper West Side apartment to celebrate a writer I don't know, have never actually read and would more than likely never get around to reading. The literary agent we happen to share, Marianna Dodson, has wangled me an invitation. Though I have never heard her say so, Marianna believes that no opportunity to further one's career, however marginal, should be left unexplored. On the other hand, my own checkered history suggests that the only good things that come to you are those you refuse to pursue.

Anyway, the party is not my first choice for the evening (probably not even my second), but out of a conspiracy of circumstances (not worth mentioning here) I find myself weaving my way through the wall-to-wall crowd looking for a familiar face.

My game plan, if you will, is to hang out for an hour or so, make the rounds, and find someone, a woman preferably, to join me for dinner.

So I am holding a flute of champagne above my head like an Olympic torch, eavesdropping on a conversation about the decline of civility in New York City, when I notice over the speaker's shoulder a tall, self-consciously elegant, silver-haired woman in an all black one of a kind no doubt outfit, observing me with a wry smile. I nod at her in gratuitous acknowledgment, and she winks in return. She is not someone I am likely to know so I assume that she has mistaken me for another. I tend at times to be confused with a sanctimonious, high-profile trial lawyer who specializes in controversial cases.

A moment later, the exquisitely overdressed fiftyish woman appears mysteriously at my side. I offer my name and hold out my hand, which you studiously ignore.

"I know who you are," you say. "You probably won't remember— in fact, I'm sure you won't—but you once promised you would never forget me."

"Is that right?" I say. "If I gave you a promise, I suppose I'll have to make good on it."

"Well," you say, giving me a skeptical look. "I'll give you three guesses."

The moment you appear from nowhere at my side, a name I barely remember knowing elbows itself into mind, but I immediately distrust the perception.

My first impression, I have to admit, is not overwhelmingly favorable. I find myself resenting your self-satisfied poise while I admire despite myself your *sangfroid*. Of course I know you. It's just that I can't, under the duress of the moment, remember your name.

I study your expensive face, which seems almost vulnerable in repose, and the same unlikely perception thrusts itself into consciousness again. So with overcompensating bravura and minimal conviction, I whisper for your attention alone the only name memory allows me.

I await your disappointment.

For an extended moment, you keep me on edge by saying nothing, your face masking your thoughts and then, as if lifting the curtain on a performance, you offer an amused smile. "I was beginning to doubt my own existence," you say.

Once your name is in the air between us, I remember with a kind of total recall our first meeting. It was at a wedding of mutual friends that we met for the first time and it was true, as you claimed, that I had told you—I had been very young, young for my age, when I made the pronouncement—that I would never forget you.

*   *   *

Joshua and Genevieve had written their own vows and Josh, wearing glasses I'd never seen on him before, read his statement from note cards. We had been friends since high school and much of the substance of his statement I had heard before. "When Genevieve and I broke up for the third time," he confided to his wedding guests, "I was absolutely sure it was over. In fact, it was a year after our third agreement to call it quits before we even talked to each other again. One of us called—it was me, I have to say—to break the silence. And the other, which would have to be Genevieve, said, 'You don't know how much I was hoping you'd call,' and then I said, 'Not half as much as I was hoping you'd say that.'"

*   *   *

I noticed out of the side of my eye that the woman standing to my right had a storm of tears streaming down her face.

Not knowing what else to say, I asked (a little foolishly, I admit) if you were all right.

Even as the tears continued to fall, you put a finger over your lips to silence me.

Annoyed at your rebuke, distracted from the ceremony, I turned away, but then I found myself glancing at you again. You had the kind of charismatic presence certain film actors have only in front of the camera. For the moment, I was your camera and I was so entranced by your charm I didn't hear a word of Genevieve's statement. Even when I looked elsewhere, anywhere else, you were there, your shimmering aura in my mind's eye.

"I'm in love," I remember saying to myself, a joke really because I would not allow myself to believe it, exorcising the demon before it took hold. The translation of my feelings seemed to pass through three or four obscure languages. "I want to be with her" was the only message I allowed myself.

"She's taken," I was later told by Josh's mother who had come up to me after the ceremony. "She's living with someone, a man named Roger, I'm told."

And I had not even asked at that point. Was there something in my face that conveyed the question?

That they all seemed to know I was pursuing you made it somehow easier as if it wasn't my choice to behave badly, merely the nature of the character I had been assigned to play.

"You nearly drowned us all in there," I said to you, looking for something to say.

You laughed, which was a generous response to an awkward remark, and it gave me a rush of pleasure. "Don't you know when a woman cries at a wedding, you're supposed to look the other way," you said. "I have this way of identifying with all the participants at these affairs—bride, groom, maid of honor, caterers, mothers, former lovers."

"Hey, and there I was identifying with you when you were crying," I said.

You squeezed my arm, our first intimacy. "You weren't really, were you?" you said. "You weren't ... If you were, you wouldn't have asked if I was all right."

I managed by switching the table cards to sit next to you during the dinner, and we hung out together, even danced a couple of times at the reception that followed.

Afterwards, expecting to be turned down, I invited you as casually as fear of rejection allowed to go out with me for a nightcap. You looked behind you to see who might be listening before saying,

"Sounds good," punctuated by a sassy laugh. The fact of the live-in boyfriend had come up earlier, reference to his being in Chicago on business, though no mention had been made of him since that initial establishing of your unavailability.

A rapport had been struck between us, a kind of misleading ease, and I remember the flickering self-protective thought that this was just an idle flirtation, that in all likelihood nothing was going to happen between us.

* * *

"You look very much the same," you say

"Why don't we go some place we can talk," I say. "There's a Starbucks around the corner, I believe."

"There's a Starbucks around every corner," you say. "Anyway, my husband will be here in about five minutes to pick me up."

"Is the husband you're meeting the guy, what's his name, Roger, the guy you were with when we met?"

"My husband's name is Tom," you say.

"Whatever happened to what's his name … Roger?"

"Whatever happened happened. Obviously we moved out of each others' lives. That was twenty-seven years ago. I have trouble remembering what happened last week."

"Hey, I hung out by the phone for months, gave up eating and sleeping, hoping to hear you had broken with Roger."

"Hey yourself," you say. "You didn't. You know you didn't. I suppose I assumed you had also moved on. Or maybe there was something about you that scared me."

At that point, my agent, Marianna Dodson, intrudes, appropriates my arm, announcing that there is someone interesting she wants me to meet.

"I'm meeting someone interesting now," I say, introducing you, though it appears you already know each other.

"We can talk later," you say.

I let myself be led away, and in another room I am introduced to an editor who has just been rewarded with her own imprint and is looking, so Marianna whispers in my ear, for something important to launch her list.

"I really liked your early stuff," the editor tells me. "The book you wrote about the First World War, what was the name of it again, it stayed with me for the longest time. If you have something like that on the way, I'd love to have the opportunity to look at it."

I am working on a novel that I still don't understand about the lost memory of an event that may or may not have ever taken place, and it seems somewhere between a year and forever away from completion. So as not to embarrass Marianna, I thank the editor for her interest and promise to think of her when the book is ready to show.

All of that takes ten minutes and I move on under the guise of getting myself another glass of champagne, retracing my steps to see if you are still around. You are not where you were.

I escape from another conversation, discard the champagne I hadn't really wanted and I wander through the adjoining two rooms, assuming with more annoyance than regret that the husband I continue to think of as Roger has come for you and you have returned to the life you have been living for almost thirty years without me.

I make an effort to talk to other people while glancing around whatever room I am in in the vain hope that you will mysteriously reappear.

* * *

The Village bar I took you to was predictably noisy and I suggested we move on to my apartment which was only a few blocks away. When we got to the door of my building—we had been holding hands as we walked—you stopped me and said, "Maybe this isn't such a good idea."

"What do you suggest?" I remember myself saying, resigned to the evening's uneventful conclusion.

"I should get home," you said. "Well, since we're here, I'll have one last drink for the road, then catch a cab."

As soon as we stepped inside my apartment, you leaned into me and we kissed fiercely, rattling against the door which had not yet fully closed.

It embarrassed me that my bed was unmade, but you didn't seem to mind and afterward when you did bring it up it became an edgy joke between us.

We were both besotted, as I remember it, and our lovemaking was oddly dreamlike as if we were watching two other people go at it with a kind of desperation offering itself as passion.

When you were no longer in my bed, I felt an unreasonable sense of loss.

My comprehension of the world when I was in my 20's tended to be self-involved. You wouldn't have made love to me with such abandon, I told myself (though possibly abandon was the wrong word) if you were in love with Roger. I repeated this willed perception to myself like a mantra until it seemed undeniable.

Unable to hold out, I called you at work the next day, foraging the number from the phone book. When I finally reached you, you sounded skittish, said it wasn't a good time to talk, that you would get back to me later in the week.

Two days passed without a return call and I called again, suggesting that we meet for a drink after work. "I can't," you said, then added, "I don't want to hurt Roger; can you understand?"

I spent hours replaying your response in my head, analyzing its implications. Your remark about not wanting to hurt Roger meant, as I understood it, that I was the one you really cared about. My confidence rose and fell and rose again like stock market quotes in a shaky season.

I composed a note, which I mailed to you at work, regretting its excesses as soon as the mailbox stole it from my hand.

"…" I wrote, "you remain with me like internal weather. Tell me you feel nothing for me and I won't bother you again."

"I can't tell you that," you wrote back. And the day after that, I got a note from you saying, "This is hard for me too."

* * *

You come up to me from nowhere as if you had materialized from smoke. "It was good running into you again," you say, smiling your apologetically ironic smile.

"Oh I thought you had gone," I say, on the far side of disappointed.

"As you can see, I'm still here," you say.

"Look," I say, "why didn't you call me when you broke up with Roger?"

A rumpled white-haired man appears and you introduce him as your husband, Tom. There is something familiar about him, though I don't remember the particulars of any previous encounter.

"Are you about ready to go?" Tom asks you. "This seems more like a wake than a party, doesn't it?"

"About ready," you say. "Getting there."

"I'll get myself a glass of something," Tom says, and moves off toward the back room where an assistant editor or intern is serving the California champagne.

For a moment, we have nothing to say to each other. "I'm sorry about all the questions," I say to fill the silence. "When I get obsessive about something, I have difficulty letting it go."

"If you like, we could meet for lunch some time," you say. You take a card from your purse and slip it into my jacket pocket like a magician's trick . "Call me, and we'll arrange something. Friends tell me I'm hard to reach so don't get discouraged."

You had stopped returning my calls and you hadn't answered the last two of my notes. What could I say or do, or not do, that would get you to see me again? There had to be something and I was mostly confident that eventually I would figure out what that elusive something was.

You were an honorable person, I told myself, or aspired to be (as I was myself, at least in theory), who wouldn't betray a commitment (a second time) unless you were prepared (as I half-hoped) to break with Roger altogether.

Though full of myself then, I had a way of inventing negative scenarios that protected me from the risk of rejection. What if, I worried, you broke up with Roger over me and you and I got together and, as happens, what seemed like love turned out to be something considerably less enduring. I would feel responsible, I would be responsible, for messing up your life.

Still, said the other side in the in-head debate, if you didn't love Roger (and I had to believe you didn't), wouldn't I be doing you a service by extricating you from a relationship that could only lead to grief?

Desperate to see you again, I finally decided, after rejecting the idea several times, that the only way to make my case effectively was to risk waiting for you after work.

* * *

We meet for lunch in an out of the way Vietnamese restaurant in the East Village. You are already there when I arrive, reading a book to pass the time, looking as self-possessed as ever. Before I sit down across from you, we acknowledge the occasion by shaking hands like diplomats from hostile countries.

After we order, you say, "I have a favor to ask of you. Could we not talk about the past?"

What is there between us if not the past? "Why did you suggest we get together for lunch?"

You let my question hang in the air for a while before answering. "Why do you think?" you say.

"If I knew, I wouldn't have asked," I say. "It must be as obvious to you as it is to me that our lives have gone in very different directions."

"I don't agree," you say. "It means something, it has to, that after all these years we run into each other again."

"If that means something," I say, "then what does it mean that we haven't run into each other before?"

"I've spent at least half of the last twenty-five years abroad," you say, as if that settled the matter.

"Doing what?"

"Never mind," you say. "I'm a little embarrassed to say what I came here to say because I have no idea how you're going to take it."

"Have you been married before?" I ask.

"It doesn't matter," you say.

"Everything matters," I say. "I give you my word that nothing you tell me in confidence will appear in my novel."

Again silence. "Look, there's really nothing to tell," you say. "I do some charity work. I'm on the board of a few cultural organizations and such. I'm one of those people with a bad conscience who does what she can to make herself useful. Since Tom's job brought us back to the States, I've begun painting again, which is important to me. Is that what you want to know? If we're going to be friends, you're going to have to respect that I don't like to talk about things that no longer matter. Roger, who seems to concern you more than he does me, is very old news, barely a footnote in my life. The only thing that matters, I've come to believe, is what happens next. Does that make sense to you?"

It doesn't, but I'm not prepared to say so. "OK," I say. "What happens next?"

* * *

I waited more than two hours for you in a persistent drizzle to come out of work. In retrospect, an embarrassing admission.

It seemed noble somehow—I was hoping to impress you with my steadfastness—not to seek cover. For whatever reason, you didn't appear. Perhaps you had stayed home from work that day. Perhaps you had seen me from the window and gone out the back way. Anyway, I was soaked and shivering when I got home and I felt foolish and angry and more than a little sorry for myself.

I let a week pass and then wrote you another letter, pleading for five minutes of your company, some kind of closure, not mentioning the fiasco in the rain.

I got no answer. For weeks my obsession with you deformed my life.

I was late for appointments or forgot them altogether, got into a pointless argument with a supervisor at work, broke off with a woman I'd been dating on and off for almost a year. Nevertheless, when anyone asked, I confidently announced that my infatuation with you was a thing of the past.

The first of our illicit encounters is on a Wednesday at the Plaza and we make love rather warily that second first time as if auditioning for roles we hope to be assigned.

This is the start of a series of late afternoon Wednesday liaisons, most of them at the Plaza, all of them at your behest.

One of the conditions for our weekly encounters is that I ask no questions about your life and offer as little information as possible about mine. Nevertheless, on occasion, in the most casual way, almost as if you were talking to yourself, you let slip off-handed news about your husband's tastes, mention plays the two of you have seen together, refer to movies you deplored that Tom enjoyed.

It seems to me for a while at least that I am the more secretive one. I never mention that I am also married, though living apart, separated but not quite divorced.

I am not sure what to make of our two hour a week routine. It seems an interlude, pleasurable certainly, not something I would want to give up, that exists outside my real life. I see it as a con-solation for what we didn't have twenty-seven years ago when something real may have been at stake.

Then one afternoon, an hour or so before our standing appointment, you call me at work to say you can't make it today, no explanation offered, barely an apology. It is the first call I have gotten from you since the surprise of your invitation to lunch.

*　　*　　*

Whatever my public story, I had difficulty accepting that your resolve not to see me was unalterable. For a long time, I continued to fantasize about you, imagined you calling to say you had broken with Roger, imagined us running toward each other on a crowded street, knocking people out of the way though never quite connecting. In one of my private scenarios, you would invite me over to your place (Roger mysteriously away), but then we would sit in silence, sometimes across from one another, sometimes side by side, tongue-tied with astonishment.

When I couldn't imagine you back into my bed, I started dating again—a married woman (unhappily married, she said without saying)—and I gradually stopped obsessing about what I might have done, and didn't, to get you back.

*　　*　　*

It isn't that you're the only woman in my life or that I'm smitten with you, or that our Wednesday afternoon fucking is indispensable to my wellbeing. At least, that's my understanding of the situation until the moment after your first cancellation. It is human nature no doubt that when something (or someone) becomes unavailable its value becomes immediately enhanced. So my disappointment at not seeing you this Wednesday is not to be made too much of. The odd thing is that I have been aware of resenting that you made all the arrangements (mostly all) for our assignations, assuming that I would go along with your plans. Recently, I've even imagined a scenario where I decided at the last minute not to show up.

Instead, you are the first to cancel, and when it happens it takes me a fretful hour or two to figure out what else I might do with my unsubscribed evening. I choose a movie at the Angelica to fill this hole in my day—something much admired which I haven't gotten around to yet—but I walk out before it's over, impatient with what seems to me its basic dishonesty.

In bed that night, out of favor with the gods of sleep, I rehearse in my head an inconclusive conversation we had the week before, you asking what our once a week lovemaking means to me, insisting you want an honest reply.

"I like being with you," I hear myself say.

"Yes?"

"And you?" I ask out of a sense of the obligation to reciprocate, not really wanting an answer.

"It's something I need to do for myself," you say.

"What is it that you need to do for yourself?" I ask. "Have illicit sex or have illicit sex with me?"

*   *   *

The next week when we get together, I ask you how you spent your time without me.

"My husband was sick," you say. "He asked me to stay with him."

I let the news sink in, wondering if I feel jealous of the husband whose name I somehow think of as Roger.

After the lost week, it is as if our bodies need to get acquainted with each other all over again. When you are dressing in your dreamy, painstaking way as prelude to going home, you say, "I can sense that you're beginning to get tired of me. We need to find another hotel or someone's empty apartment. A change of scenery. What do you think?"

"Last week, when you told me you weren't coming," I say, "my life felt empty. I felt unbearably deprived."

You turn your face away in what I take to be a gesture of contempt.

"Do you know," you say, "that's the first affectionate thing you've said to me." Tears rain down your face in profusion as they had when you stood next to me at Joshua and Genevieve's wedding.

I say your name as if I were an amnesiac recovering a lost fragment of memory.

Lying under the covers, I watch you as if you were a character in a movie, as you open the door in your purposeful way to leave me for wherever it is you go when you disappear. You turn to glance at me as an afterthought. "Will you choose the place for next week?" you ask.

I imagine I answer you, but in fact I say nothing, watching the door close between us. "I stood two hours in the rain for you," I say to the closed door, then I get out of bed and into my clothes, making sure ten minutes had elapsed (we are careful not to leave at the same time) before I exit the hotel and return by subway to my apartment.

* * *

To some degree, I've had to take on faith that you were the same woman I met at Joshua and Genevieve's wedding twenty-seven years ago. Of course there are certain similarities, but I read them as merely circumstantial. It's the crying for no apparent reason—the only flaw in what I think of as your perfect cool—that alters my perspective. It is as though a spell had been cast that turned you into an unrecognizable older woman and now the spell has been broken. You are once again the princess-stranger I imagined I couldn't live without almost half a lifetime ago.

I am not without resources of self-protection. I know that to fall in love with you is a sure way to lose you and I make an effort to seem as self-possessed and untouched as performance allows.

One evening you announce in bed that you are going to Prague for two weeks with Tom. "Will you miss me?" you ask as if the question amuses you.

"Why do you have to go?" I say.

"Don't you think we could do with a break?" you say, getting out of bed. "Anyway, Tom asked me to go with him and it's a chance to see a place I've never been to before. So."

I come up behind you as you are putting your sweater on over your head. "A hug for the road," I say. "Something to last me for two weeks."

You move out of my grasp before I am ready to give you up.

"It makes my jumpy when you're affectionate," you say. "I feel you take our Wednesday afternoon love nest pretty much for granted. I suspect while I'm away, you'll wonder from time to time what whatshername is doing wherversheis. You're a nice man, at least I think you are, but living in New York all these years has made you jaded."

"Has it?"

"I like that about you," you say. "I really do." You blow me a kiss at the door and then hesitate as if waiting for me to say something.

Afraid that I'll never see you again, an odd, wholly impractical idea comes to mind. "What if ...," I start to say. What if I followed you to Prague and ...

*   *   *

I know that you return on Sunday and wonder, expecting nothing, if you'll find some way to get in touch. Two days pass without word and then you leave a cryptic message on my home phone about calling you after ten the following morning.

I finally reach you at noon moments before you have to leave on some unexplained errand. "We need to talk," you say.

You make arrangements to meet me for lunch the next day at the same Vietnamese restaurant we dined at when you suggested the affair.

The portents are not difficult to read. We could have had the same talk at our hotel room at the Plaza before or after making love if something else wasn't in the wind. Choosing the Vietnamese place provides a kind of symmetry. Only a fool wouldn't recognize that this is your way of calling an end to whatever it is that's been going on between us. My first impulse is to preempt your move by striking first, but it seems a childish gesture despite its obvious satisfactions.

The real question, the one I have evaded all these months, is what do I want beyond maintaining the status quo. I confess to myself that I don't know. Ambivalence is, and has been, my MO. And even if I do know, even if I am ready (and I am not) to press you to leave your husband, what's his name, it will surely do me no good.

*   *   *

The substance of our talk over lunch is not what I spend a mostly sleepless night anticipating. What you want, what you say you want, is not to stop seeing me but to change the day of our assignations. Wednesdays are no longer possible for you. Monday evening, 5 to 7ish, is suddenly your only available time. The news brings a mixture of relief and unaccountable disappointment.

That's fine, I'm ready to say, but then I remember that I have my tennis game Monday nights, which has entailed renting a court for the indoor season. Beyond the obligation to show up, it is a great pleasure for me to play. "Monday won't work," I say.

"I was afraid of that," you say. "There's no way—I shouldn't even ask you this—you can shift things around?"

"Not really," I say. "What about you?"

You offer an exasperated sigh. "You have no idea, my friend," you say, "how difficult it's been for me to see you as I have. What is it that you do on Monday nights that's so important?"

The imperiousness in your tone annoys me and, though I want to make peace, want our routine to continue, I feel it a matter of pride to hold my ground. "It's an obligation," I say.

"Yes?" you say. "To whom?"

"I have this tennis game Monday nights," I say. "There are three other people who rely on me to be there."

"A tennis game? A tennis game! I don't know what to say."

As you rise stiffly from your chair, I put my hand on your arm to restrain you. "Please don't leave," I say. "We'll find another time that suits us both."

"I don't know that I want to see you again," you say, returning my hand to me. It is as if we are moving in different universes or perhaps a willed indifference keeps me from running after you. Whatever it is, you are out of the restaurant and into a cab before I can settle the bill (someone has to pay it) and pursue you to no avail.

We hardly ever fought even about inconsequential things before and suddenly we are locked in our first life-and-death fight. I'm willing to sacrifice tennis for you, but it seems virtually impossible now to yield to your demands since I have already drawn my line in the sand. Haven't you been unreasonable too? You haven't bothered to tell me what unbreakable commitments on your side prevent us meeting some other time.

I let a day pass to get some perspective on my feelings and then I call you at home at a time your husband is usually at work. I get your answering machine and mumble something unintelligible before hanging up in despair.

The next time I call—I let two days pass before I try again—you pick up, but you don't stay on the line long enough to hear me out, though I'm aware, even while pleading for your forgiveness, that the things I'm willing to say are not what you want to hear. When I think about our standoff, which is all I do, it strikes me that I have more reason to be angry at you than you at me, but such wisdom seems idle comfort.

* * *

A further irony: I pull something in my back playing tennis and I have to take a month off from the game.

And then one day, six months or so after our misunderstanding, you call me at home on a Saturday afternoon.

You identify yourself, though of course I know immediately that it's you. "How are you?" you ask.

"Much better now that I hear your voice," I say.

Your laugh sounds as if it has been rehearsed. "I'm really calling to say goodbye," you say. "My husband's firm is moving him back to the London office and we leave at the end of the month. As a matter of fact, we leave in four days."

"Four days," I repeat, trying to remember if you ever told me what it is he does. "For how long?"

"You never know," you say. "It could be forever for all anyone knows."

"That's a long time," I say. "Well, I hope it's what you want."

"Thank you for that," you say. "Look, I'm free, or can be, on Tuesday at about 5 and I wonder if we could meet at the Plaza."

The unholy surprise of your offer astonishes me into a protracted silence.

"If you can't make it," you say, "I'll pretend to be understanding."

"I can make it," I say.

My acceptance creates a momentary silence on your end. "Well, good," you say. "I've reserved our old room."

* * *

It is not our old room after all, but the one directly above, which has certain similarities and as such seems disconcertingly dreamlike.

You are uncharacteristically late and it strikes me—I tend to expect the worst—that you might still be angry and decide not to show up. These anxious feelings persist even after your arrival.

"Damn," you say, putting on your glasses for confirmation, "everything's changed." We remain in our clothes for awhile, one of us sitting on the bed, the other in an overstuffed chair across the room.

"It doesn't make any sense," you say, "but I'm feeling shy. It's not only that we haven't seen each other in a while; it's something else altogether. Do you have any idea what I'm talking about?"

"You know we don't have to make love," I say. "We can just sit and talk."

"What should we talk about," you say. And I have the sense that if I say anything at this point, you'll put on your coat and go home.

I shrug and offer what I hope is a comforting smile.

"What should we talk about?" you say again. "You know sometimes I don't understand you at all. Is that what you want to come to the Plaza with me for the last time not to make love?"

You seem about to cry and I will myself to move toward you and end up kneeling awkwardly beside your chair, the forgotten ache in my back making an unexpected return.

"How much I hated you these past months," you say. "You can't possibly imagine. I even thought of running you over in a rented car when you were coming out of your damn tennis club."

I put my head in your lap and you say, "Is this what you think I want," abruptly tugging at my hair, and for that moment, I regret forgiving you, I regret giving in to your whims, I regret being here with you when we have no future. As I'm about to say, "I don't need this from you," you lean toward me and kiss my eyes. "I hate you," you whisper. "I will hate you for as long as we both shall live."

"Those sound like wedding vows," I say.

"Are you making fun of me? Is that what it's come to?"

I lift you to your feet and we dance—you in your heels, me in my stocking feet—to whatever music the silence provides.

When we finally get under the covers, I notice from the clock on the wall that we have less than an hour left us. I imagine the hour passing, imagine our fucking, which is more tender than usual, though not quite as intense as it has been at its best. I imagine you getting into your clothes, that refined and complicated ritual, while I consider pleading with you to stay five minutes longer. I imagine watching you from the hotel window as you get into a waiting cab and drive off to your husband, whom I envision as a shadow figure. Then I imagine the two of you, you and the shadow husband, boarding a flight for London. Then I imagine getting older and being alone and trying to remember this last time together, which has passed with so little moment.

It is only then when I have already imagined the end of whatever has gone on between us, that we begin to make love—we have been holding each other carefully, cautiously—and it seems like the first time, which I don't actually remember, which I confuse with a number of other first times, but I allow myself to imagine that we are in my old Village apartment in my unmade bed and that it hurts me that you live with a man named Roger (though I know you don't love him) and whatever is happening between us (sex no doubt, terrifying intimacy, the compelling illusion of love) will go on for as long as I can imagine it going on, for as long as consciousness and self-deception and the trick of memory survives.

THREE

———

I tend to feel claustrophobic in elevators even when I'm the only passenger, especially so when I'm imprisoned by myself. My imagination tends to betray me. I anticipate getting stuck somewhere between floors, trapped in an airless space for an extended, open-ended piece of time. So meeting you or anyone in an elevator is an unlikely circumstance for someone who rides only when there is no other choice. The rickety elevator in this old Upper West Side building—my friends the Powers live on the fourteenth floor (there is no thirteenth, its own example of omen-phobia)—does not inspire confidence.

So I am prepared to trudge down twelve flights when I notice you waiting, sparks of impatience floating around your head like an aura, for the ancient elevator to hurtle noisily upward in its death-defying slow-motion to take you down, and I make a rapid reassessment of my options. You ignore my presence and continue to stare determinedly at the elevator doors.

"Waiting long?" I ask.

"Forever," you say, barely glancing at me as if the elevator's arrival depended on your impatient vigil.

When it arrives, I casually follow you in just as the doors begin to close.

Not wanting to intrude, I stand at least three feet away, waiting with disguised anxiety in my own separate but unequal universe for the elevator to release us again into the world.

During our endless (or so it seems) plummet to earth, I rehearse silently in almost infinite variation an invitation to you to go off with me for a drink.

The performance, though rehearsed to a fault, never gets to play before its intended audience.

We each in turn refuse to violate the silence.

When we separate you say, "Nice to have met you," though in fact we have never met, have never been introduced, have only exchanged glances across a crowded room.

I call out my name to your back as you dash off, and as you wave to a taxi that actually stops at your signal.

* * *

The next time we get together it is in another elevator in a building no more than seven blocks from the first for another party, this time ascending. You seem less preoccupied, less unhappy, and you introduce yourself as if we had never seen each other before.

"Weren't you at the Powers a few weeks ago?" I say.

"Oh were you there too?" you say, studying my face. "Yes, I believe I remember seeing you. You have the face of a pirate."

"A pirate? What do you mean, a pirate?"

"That was the thing that struck me about you," you say. "It's a good look really. I wouldn't let it worry you."

This is a much quicker elevator than the one in the Powers' building and we are at our floor before I can come up with an appropriate response.

At the party itself, you wink at me the few times I catch your eye, but we never actually get to talk.

I leave early, having somewhere else to go, carrying with me (what else is there to do with it?) your incomprehensible pirate remark. No one has ever told me that I look like a pirate before. That night, I study my face in the bathroom mirror, looking for clues to what you think you see.

This is what I discover. I discover that I like the idea that you imagine I look like a pirate because even after my extended acquaintance with my reflection, I see none of it. Well, maybe something of it—the bags under the eyes, the sour turn of the mouth, the all-day 4 o'clock shadow. Is that the way a pirate looks? I don't know if I've ever knowingly seen a pirate outside of the movies.

I become counter-phobic about elevators, riding them at every opportunity, an imaginary pirate-like bravado driving me, hoping to run into you again in our favored place of encounter.

If it happens, or rather when it happens, I will say that you look like a princess that any self-respecting pirate would like to ride off with in his pirate ship. Of course that can't be said without embarrassing us both. Something will come to mind I tell myself.

*   *   *

I am riding up in an elevator to see my father, who lives on the fifth floor of a twelve-floor building, and when the elevator opens to let me out (it hesitates just enough to give a seasoned pirate pause), you are there waiting to enter.

"Hello," I say, and again you don't seem to recognize me.

"We've met before, haven't we?" you say. "I know we have. It wasn't at college, was it?"

I hold the door for you as you enter and in turn, you hold it for me as I take your place on the other side, the door sliding shut between us.

"You said I looked like a pirate," I shout impulsively at the closed door just as the elevator begins its descent. I imagine I hear the echo of your laugh, or someone's laugh, and I consider for an abortive moment running down the steps to meet you as you land.

Once I've pursued you in conjectured scenario, the pursuit itself, the flight down the stairs, seems anticlimactic. So I don't get off the mark, regretting in advance the missed opportunity.

As a rule, after my visit with my father, needing to reclaim my separateness, I walk down the four flights to the street. On this occasion, however, I ride the elevator, braving the danger, in the unadmitted hope of another chance encounter.

In my experience, anticipation inevitably denies possibility. When the elevator arrives to pick me up, there is no other passenger, not you, not anyone like you, inside waiting to get out.

So I have my head down, am without expectation, when the elevator deposits me on the first floor. A man with a large black dog takes my place in the elevator and I make my way to the outside door, nodding to the security guy as I pass his post, trying to visualize where exactly I parked my car.

"Hello there," someone says to me, the almost familiar voice intruding on my private despair.

When I look up, you are standing to my right, carrying a bag of groceries, waiting for me to acknowledge you.

It takes me a moment to pull myself free from the quicksand of distraction. I nod gravely, acknowledging your fortuitous presence as if it were some kind of divine omen. And this time it is you who announce that we've met before, the details (a few of them) unexpected news.

And for a moment, awaking from my own self-involved scenario, I find myself lost in yours. "So you live in this building," I say.

"Oh no," you say, put off apparently by my preferring the obvious conclusion to the unimaginable. "I'm staying with a friend while my place is being renovated."

While assessing the implications of your information, I make some awkward consoling remark about knowing from personal experience the trials of dislocation.

"Did I ever tell you," you say, politely ignoring my banalities, "that you look like a pirate?"

We are now perhaps for the first time on the same page, but I pretend never to have heard this inexplicable perception from you before. "A pirate?" I say.

You reassess me, squinting your eyes to get an unambiguous view. "I said this to you before, didn't I?" you say.

I want to ask, but don't, whether it's acceptable or not to resemble a pirate or even what it might mean in the general scheme of things. "Does that mean you are afraid of me?" I ask.

You smile, barely, shift your feet, seem prepared to face dangers far more threatening than any I may represent. "I really have to get these groceries upstairs. It was nice seeing you again."

"Would you like me to help you with the bag," I say.

"Thank you for the offer," you say, "but I don't think it's such a good idea. I'll be back in my own place by next Friday unless the job takes longer than they say. I suppose everything does, right?" You take a small card from your purse—a reminder card for a dental appointment—and write down a phone number on the back.

After that, we shake hands as if some kind of treaty has been concluded, and go our separate ways. The elevator, I notice, arrives at the behest of a man my father's age, who holds the door for you as you slip inside, and you are already in flight before I have enough self-possession to toss you the shards of my name.

*   *   *

Anyway, I have the name of your dentist and the time of your next appointment, which opens up another way of getting together circumstantially.

It turns out that I am between dentists at the moment, my most recent guy, Dr. F, having retired abruptly for undisclosed reasons.

I keep your card on my dresser, dental side down, and plan to call you when the week is out—I even make a notation on my desk calendar to phone you three days after your scheduled return—but it doesn't happen.

I decode my reasons, which are unconvincing even to me, and may be understood as follows. The friend you have been staying with who lives in the same building as my father and apparently on the same floor is, more than likely, more than just a friend. Therefore: what?

I don't call because I don't want to trespass on a preexisting relationship and so become the agency of conflict and grief in your life. That can't be true, but my reading of my resistance to using the number you gave me yields no deeper truth.

Instead of calling you, I turn over your card and make an appointment to see your dentist. On my arrival, I am given a questionnaire to fill out concerning the highlights of my dental history. The last question asks the name of the person whose recommendation has brought me to this office.

What's it to them? I wonder, though I give them your name in case some free service is offered—a gift filling perhaps—for each new patient brought to their door.

The hygienist is particularly brutal and complains throughout the treatment about the extent of my bleeding as if some failure of character were at issue. Before the dentist is brought in for the heavy lifting, she insists on giving me a lesson on flossing.

"How do you know my sister?" she asks.

I can't answer of course, can only sit mystified in my supine position in her chair, until she gets her floss and fingers out of my mouth.

"Your sister?" I say. "Why would I know your sister?"

"When you floss," you say, "it's good thing to hold a mirror in front of you so you can see yourself flossing. Her name, you wrote her name on your questionnaire as your referral to Dr. Karsik, We're actually half-sisters."

At this point, the bespectacled Dr. K, the dentist we now share, makes his first appearance on the scene. While inspecting my mouth, he keeps up a running stream of conversation with the hygienist, a kind of flirtation disguised and enhanced by insult.

In the process, Dr. Karsik discovers two cavities, one barely emerging and the other in the need of immediate attention.

So I make an appointment before leaving to return a different day the following week to have the more desperate of my two cavities attended to before matters get out of hand.

* * *

A week or so before my return to your dentist, I actually run into you getting out of a subway train at Columbus Circle. This time we are both getting off at the same stop, though we make our almost simultaneous getaways from different cars of the same train.

You are ahead of me and hurrying somewhere and I try to keep you in sight without giving the unavoidable appearance of running after you.

And then someone else stops me to say hello, a former flame (whose name I can't quite remember), whom I haven't seen in what I estimate to be ten years. We exchange phone numbers and highlights of recent history and continue, our interlude concluded, on our separate ways.

Nevertheless the encounter, which takes no more than three minutes, is sufficient for me to lose sight of you as you hurry to keep some unimaginable appointment.

Well, perhaps it is imaginable, your destination. You were hurrying uptown in the direction of—why hasn't this struck me before?—Lincoln Center. It's likely that you are going to see a matinee and all I have to do is figure out where you might be going out of a handful of possibilities.

By the time I reach Lincoln Center, my enthusiasm for the game of finding you has lost its edge.

There are only two matinees, as it turns out, and a critics screening for the upcoming film festival. One out of three is better odds than I might have imagined, but on the other hand I have no basis for choice.

Anyway, I have a day pass for the new Rohmer film awaiting me at the press desk, so I pick it up (at first they can't find it, another delay) and I enter the dark auditorium a few minutes after "The Lady and the Duke" has started.

At some point in the proceedings—there's the usual elbow-tilting with my neighbor for the armrest—it strikes me that even if you are at the screening it won't be a walk in the park to find you among the dispersing crowd.

And then I think, the woman next to me on the right, the one with the aggressive elbow, might possibly be you. I like that idea and I hold on to it, imagine my feigned surprise at discovering you next to me.

The movie, like many of Rohmer's, though uncharacteristically set in the past (during the Reign of Terror following the French Revolution), is about noble (and ignoble) self-deceptions.

Before the lights go on, as the credits unroll, I slide out of the aisle and hang out with my back to the wall. You come out of my row—you were in fact the elbow on my right—and I am about to say something when I realize you are with the man trailing you and it is—he is—somebody I know.

You ignore me, but he comes over to say hello and provides, somewhat belatedly, our first third person introduction.

I take my cue from you, that is I pretend we don't know each other, though it also strikes me that you have not remembered me (the pirate?) as your traveling companion on several elevator rides.

We shake hands in this formal way as if parodying the ritual.

"We're going for a bite at O'Neil's," your companion, my nodding acquaintance, Roger, says. "Why don't you join us?"

I am already uncomfortable with the situation so I drudge up a pro forma excuse, an apocryphal appointment elsewhere, to avoid further awkwardness.

"Do join us," you say. "Roger tells me you're a movie fanatic. I could use some clarity about what we just saw."

I play hard to get for no more than a few minutes before agreeing to postpone whatever else of worked-up importance I had allegedly committed myself to.

So my first meal with you, our first date so to speak, also includes Roger, who may (or may not) be the mysterious friend you were staying with while your apartment was being renovated.

During our abbreviated first date—I suppose it isn't really a date if Roger is with us—it is Roger who explains the movie to you, looking over at me from time to time as if anticipating my objection.

"So the more things change, the more they remain the same," Roger says in conclusion.

"Isn't that what you think everything's about?" you say. "I think it's about their loving each other and not being able to admit it even to themselves."

"What I said includes what you said," he says.

"That's because it's general enough to include almost everything," you say.

I say virtually nothing during the meal, listen to your dispute as if I were an invisible eavesdropper.

At some point, Roger reminds me that (in case I'd forgotten) I have a prior appointment to keep and that they would understand my having to, as they say, eat and run.

So what can I do but put on my jacket, say goodbye, throw some money on the table, and walk away, regretting my lies.

You call after me, "You never gave us your take on the film. So?"

I wave away the question as if it hasn't quite reached me, but then I call back, unable to leave it unsaid, "I mostly agree with you."

When I get home I look for the dental card you gave me with your number on it, look in vain through the scraps of paper I keep in chaotic file on my dresser.

I know I put it on top of my dresser—it's where everything goes—and I know I haven't removed it. But it's no longer there.

I move the dresser away from the wall, look among the decade of debris behind it and then get down on my hands and knees to look under the dresser. There is something there, but it is something else—the card for my next dental appointment, which I somehow figured was still in my wallet.

* * *

The next time we meet is not in the dentist's waiting room, but in a crowded elevator at the Brooklyn Museum. You are there with another woman while I am, as usual, alone. I am wedged in the back of the huge car, regretting my decision to ride, and you are at the front of the elevator, unaware of my existence.

When the elevator deposits us on the fifth floor, I walk determinedly past you, hoping to be discovered.

I hear you say something and I turn around, thinking it is addressed to me when it is not. "I'll wait for you in the first room of the exhibit," you say (have said) to your companion who is going off to the bathroom.

"Oh hello," you say, this time to me. "Where did you come from?"

I don't know where to begin, which prompts a silence that might have extended itself into mouth-gaping embarrassment without your intercession.

"I don't seem to be able to turn around without running into you," you say.

"I might say the same thing."

"Please don't," you say. "Say something original instead."

That leaves me searching in vain for a clever comeback just long enough for your friend to return and the two of you go off in your predetermined direction before I have a chance to offer an excuse for not getting around to calling you as promised.

Your friend, Deidre, whispers something in your ear and you giggle, the sound hanging in the air as I turn away to check out the less notorious show in the other direction.

But then you return, catching me off guard, to tell me that Deidre insists that it's no fun looking at paintings of nude women without a man present.

So I end up walking through the *Exposed* show behind you and sometimes between you, my opinion assessed at virtually every painting.

"Does it induce prurient thoughts?" Deidre asks.

"No thoughts whatsoever," I say.

"Salacious suppositions perhaps?" you say. "On a scale of one to ten, how would you rate it?"

I clear my throat.

"What's that supposed to mean?" Deidre says. "I happen to think this painting is hot."

"Do you?" you say.

"As a matter of fact, I do," Deidre says. "This painting, *The Goddess's Surrender,* is, to my untrained eye, the hottest painting in the room. But what do I know—I'm just a girl."

You turn to me and wink. "Whatever you tell us," you say to me, lowering your voice, "it will not leave this museum. A show like this is no fun without a man's point of view."

"*The Goddess's Surrender* doesn't do anything for me," I say.

"I rather think," Deidre says, "that it does so much for you you're embarrassed to admit it."

"There is nothing I'm embarrassed to admit," I say, more mock bravado than outright lie.

"Then you're the boy we want with us on this trip down prurience lane," Deidre says. "You're our yardstick so to speak."

"But who's counting inches," you say—we are now in the second room—"Are you counting inches?"

"Not me," says Deidre. "What about you?"

I pick out the least exposed nude in the room to admire, a small Sichert, which earns me a Bronx cheer from Deidre.

"It's always the same story with men," Deidre says. "They pretend to know what we want but they never give it to us."

"I think the opposite is closer to the truth," you say.

"Do you?" Deidre says. "What can possibly be the opposite of my remark? Wait a minute. I think I see what you're saying."

"In that case, I wish you'd tell me what it is," you say.

"I don't want to embarrass your friend by explaining the obvious," Deidre says. "I think we're in serious danger here of crossing the imaginary line."

"Don't be so cocksure," you say. "My friend always looks a little uncomfortable even in the most unprovocative circumstances. I don't know him well enough to say this, but I don't think he embarrasses easily ... Do you ... embarrass easily?" she asks me.

"Only when asked about embarrassment," I say, more than a little uncomfortable.

"That's just something to say," Deidre says. "That's just trying to be clever in my opinion. Wouldn't you agree?"

It's not clear to whom the question is addressed.

You are not yourself in Deidre's company—that is, the you that partners with Deidre is not a you I've met before. At this point, I am looking for an escape route.

* * *

I loiter in front of a painting of a girl about fifteen, consumptively thin, wearing only a feather boa, while the two of you prance on ahead of me.

"He's less fun than frat house sex," I hear someone say in a noisy whisper, unsure which of you it is, though willing to hold Deidre responsible.

"Let's lose him," the second speaker broadcasts.

When the two of you cross over into the next (and last) room of the show, I turn around and leave the exhibition.

* * *

A few days later, early for an appointment at Dr. K's, I meet you, or rather discover you sitting behind a book, in the waiting room.

I nod in your direction and take a seat just far enough away so as to avoid you without overstating the point. Before I can open my newspaper, I realize that you are in the seat next to me.

"I don't have an appointment for today," you say. "I knew from my sister that you were going to be here. That's why I came."

"You came to the dentist to see me?" I say. "Is that what you're saying?"

"That's it," you say. "Look, I'll understand if you don't want to, but I'd be greatly pleased if you'll have a cup of coffee with me as my treat after you're done."

At that very moment, perhaps even before your sentence is completed, the receptionist calls out my name. The dentist apparently is ready to engage the cavity he had befriended on my last visit.

I wave to you as I go off, find myself in the dentist's chair, tilted back, bullets of cotton wedged in my mouth, when I realize that I hadn't actually accepted your offer.

By the time Dr. K finishes with me, the last thing I want is human company, and anyway you are not in the waiting room to meet me when I stagger out, much of my mouth still numb from the Novocain.

And then of course I am angry that you are not there after going out of your way to find me and apologize (though you haven't really apologized) and I walk to the subway with my collar up in the late afternoon chill.

Then I see you, hurrying toward me, a large shopping bag in each hand. "I almost missed you," you say. "Where should we go?"

With my mouth insensate, I have difficulty making words so I offer a sympathetic silence.

"Are you angry at me?" you ask.

I quasi shrug, quasi nod, go through the motions of shaking my head, offer more than one conflicting message.

"I want to get rid of these packages," you say. "Why don't we go to my place and I'll make us a light lunch."

I am not ready to accept your offer, or perhaps I am more than ready to accept it, and I walk along with you, our arms avoiding touch and brushing almost simultaneously, to the nearest subway.

"Look, it's too nice a day to go into the subway," you say. "Why don't we take a cab. It'll be my treat."

You don't wait for me to respond to your offer—I've not said a word in the fifteen minutes or so following my escape from the dentist's—but hail the first cab you see, which stops for us as if prearranged and before I can access my intention I am following you up the steps to your fifth floor brownstone apartment.

As you unlatch the door with your key, I glance at my watch, an habitual gesture to no purpose, which you acknowledge with a corner of the mouth smile.

Your place, not at all what I imagined, has a minimalist rooming-house demeanor and exemplifies a casual disregard for the conventional verities of middle class/bohemian taste. I need to say something to cover my surprise, which is at first negative then something else, a kind of admiration bordering on awe.

"You make interesting use of the space," I say, my speech barely intelligible, though I can feel the numbness beginning to recede.

"Do I?" you say, putting my jacket in the closet. "A lot of my stuff is still in boxes ... Do you have any food issues?"

"Issues?"

"I'm afraid I didn't get what you said," you say. "What I'm asking is, is there anything you don't eat?"

"Dirt." I say, which does not produce a smile.

In short order, you set the table in your eat-in kitchen and produce a chicken salad from the refrigerator swaddled in plastic wrap.

"Maybe we ought to wait a few minutes," I say. "The Novocain hasn't worn off yet."

You nod to yourself, seem to repress a smile, and return the chicken salad to its former exile.

* * *

I should pause here to remark that nothing happens between us—my coming to your apartment, your making me lunch, my inability to eat the chicken salad you offer—that leads or seems to lead to our going to bed together for the first time.

Nevertheless it happens even though I am unable to chart the exact course that carries us from A to B or A to C or A to Z or whatever it is that represents our interlude in your bed before or after or instead of lunch.

And so, after all the elusive elevator rides, after my long-standing tentative and failed pursuit, we get it together, we make love, as a time killer until I regain enough feeling in my mouth to get through the main agenda of lunch.

In place of lunch, the sex aside, we share a glass of white wine and a cigarette.

Afterward, when I am about to leave, you say, "Look, this won't happen again. I want you to know that so there'll be no misunderstanding down the road."

Before you say this, I am already in another place in regard to you. "Was I that much of a disappointment?" I ask.

"To the contrary," you say. "If we're going to remain friends, and I really want us to be friends, I promise you I do, you'll have to accept my terms."

"Do I get an explanation?"

"There is none," you say after a moment of what I hope might be reconsideration. "For the record—is getting into my pants the only thing that interests you about me?"

And then I have this flash that you and Deidre have set me up, that it is all prearranged including the sex, and I elect not to play your game. "The only thing," I say.

"What?" Disbelief.

I resist the impulse to explain myself, to say it is the only possible answer to your outrageous question. Instead, I collect my jacket from the closet. When I turn around, you are folded up on the couch, your head nestled into your arms like a bird, silently crying or offering your audience that impression.

I stop at the door and look back, torn between wanting to get away and wanting to comfort you.

The second option chooses me and I squat down on the edge of the couch and stroke your hair. And stroke your hair.

Finally, you lift your head in a kind of slow motion, turning it just enough to glance in my direction. "Please leave," you say.

I think of myself, dignity in hand, getting up from my corner of the couch. In my imagination I am walking to the door, unlatching it, opening it, closing it quietly behind me, bounding down the four flights of stairs to the street, hoping to outrun the depression that beggars onto my sleeve as I go.

In fact, in the unimagined world, I don't move.

FOUR

I am in your bed, your back to my side, fiddling with the Double Crostic puzzle in the Sunday *Times Magazine*, when you turn toward me, propped on an elbow (last I looked you were asleep) and say without context, "Don't you think that if you have been betrayed more than twice in your life, you have no one to blame but yourself?" You issue this provocative remark an hour or so after we have tangled, tangoed, on your Swedish bed and shortly before you confide that I am not the only man in your life.

I assume that when you make the betrayal pronouncement that you are referring to me while, as it turns out, it is about the other . "Roger gets off on being betrayed," you say. "I'm afraid his life would feel incomplete to him without it."

"Does he?" I say

"Yes, I would say so," you say.

I am about to ask why you presume to know that I have a history of being betrayed—do I? I wonder—when you confess that you have been dating this guy, Roger, off and on for over seven years. Our connection has only a nine-months duration, though I have more invested in it than I like to admit.

"Why have you brought this up now?" I ask.

"Because I hate lying and liars," you declaim as if performing before a TV camera.

"But why now? Why not after we made love for the first time? Why not last week, say?"

You rub your face against mine like a cat before answering. "I suppose I was afraid I'd lose you," you say.

Had you not brought up the issue of betrayal as such, I might have been able to accept your confession with better grace. Getting betrayed, that is knowing you've been deceived, is not easy to accept. I have been unhappily on both sides of that equilibrium.

Let's flash back to the week before when you offer me another kind of confession altogether. You mention with touching shyness as if it's a dangerous admission that you love me. You make this confession twice actually in the same night—once in the throes and again about two hours later when I reenter your bed after a turn in the bathroom.

When you tell me that you love me—the second time in particular—it is as though a windfall of grace has entered my life. And for an unguarded moment, I am aware, anxiously aware, of being happy.

It is not inconceivable that you have had a similar conversation with Roger the day before or ten months ago, which vitiates my hopeful moment, perhaps erases it altogether.

Roger is, among other things, an architect. We might have some history together, but I no longer remember what it is. You met him, you tell me, when his firm renovated your weekend house in Vermont. A wife, later to be former, was somewhere offstage.

This much is relatively clear: my role in your life is to be the unwitting agent of Roger's betrayal, for which Roger, who is addicted to being betrayed, is conveniently responsible.

All this is playing in my head when I get up from your Swedish orthopedic queen-size bed—I am wearing a T-shirt and nothing else—and put on my pants. I have no idea how angry I am until you ask why I am leaving.

"I thought I might call this other woman I haven't seen in a while," I say.

"Who is this other woman?"

"You have no reason to feel jealous," I say.

"So you say."

By the time you are up and about, I am a step from going out the door, though I am not averse to being stopped.

"I'd appreciate if you didn't leave like this," you say in your most imperious voice. "We should discuss this, don't you think?"

Momentum has its own logic. I am on the other side of your door, the door closed behind me, halfway down the first flight of stairs, a slow-motion replay of hasty retreat.

*   *   *

When I get to my place, which seems more than usually bleak, I can't imagine what possessed me to walk out on you. There's been no explicit agreement between us not to see other people.

And I've never been a jealous man as such.

I haven't even removed my jacket and I am already conjecturing a return to the scene of the crime, playing out in the imagination the soap opera scenario of my reappearance at your door.

I have a tendency, as I don't have to tell you, to visualize the consequences of an act in advance of risking it.

In one of my scenarios, the last in fact, the defining moment, if you will, a man answers my knock at the door. He is wearing one of those silky dressing gowns that gangsters and cads wore in old Hollywood movies.

If you call, which you don't, and are persuasively apologetic, which you are not (and can't be unless you call), it might make a decision to return less fraught with risk.

In the end, my decision not to return makes itself. I can't go back, not tonight, without suffering serious loss of false pride.

I realize the position I allow myself has no flexibility, yet what else can I do?

* * *

I meet you for dinner the following Saturday at a place we've never gone before. We take turns apologizing for our behavior on the night of your disturbing confession and then you say that if I ask you to stop seeing Roger, if that's what's necessary to return things between us to the way they were, you will think about it.

Your offer surprises me—it was not one of my pre-dinner scenarios—so I have to listen to it echo in my head before coming to terms with it. "OK," I say. "Yeah, sure."

My hesitation seems to disturb you. "If we make such an agreement," you say, "you're going to have to stop dating other people. Are you sure that's what you want?"

Although you are the only woman in my life at the moment, I balk momentarily at putting such an absolute restriction on my illusory freedom. Finally, I offer my hand to seal our bargain, which you accept with some hesitation of your own, giving it a parsimonious squeeze.

After dinner, we return to your apartment, which is in keeping with our usual routine, scrunch down on your familiar, not quite comfortable couch, and neck like teenagers in a car parked on a dark and silent street. Then instead of moving into the bedroom, closing the deal as it were, we get into talking in a less guarded way than usual and we both admit—you first—to distrusting somewhat the other's ability to remain faithful.

"I want to trust you," you say, "I really do, but I don't know that I can, I really don't. There's this other woman in your life and there's Roger in mine. I wonder if it's such a good idea to stop seeing others—you know what I mean?—while there's all this potential distrust between us."

"Hey, it was your idea," I say. "You said if I asked, you would stop seeing Roger."

"As usual, you're misquoting me," you say. "What I said was, if you asked me to break with Roger, I would think about it, which is what I've been doing. I'm thinking why should I give up Roger if you continue to see whoever you'be been seeing. You haven't even given me a name. Who is the woman you went to see last Saturday after you left my bed?"

"The name doesn't matter," I say, unwilling to acknowledge at this point that your rival is imaginary.

"I want a name," you say. "I want everything out in the open between us or we have no deal."

I put on my shirt and slide into my pants one leg at a time before I answer and even then, I hesitate, flirt with the idea of making up a name, which I reluctantly reject as a gesture of bad faith.

"Are you going to run out on me again?" you ask. "If you do that to me again ..." You leave the threat implied.

And then (for no reason it seems to me—perhaps because I smile, or smirk as you say), you flail at me, hitting me repeatedly in the chest, the blows without much force though cumulative in their impact.

I have to grab your wrists to get you to stop, but that only seems to fuel your rage.

"Why won't you tell me her name?" you whisper as though it were a scream. "Is she that important to you?"

"There is no name," I say. "Think about it. A name will make this person who doesn't matter to either of us memorable in a way that will make us both unhappy."

"I am already unhappy with you," you say.

We go on this way for a while, the stakes increasing as the argument deteriorates into pettiness, the realm of the unforgivable.

"I'm glad this has happened," you say, meaning the opposite or at least something else altogether. "It has definitely shown me a side of you you'd kept hidden from me and for good reason.

You always seemed kind to a fault, but that's not who you really are, is it?"

Your verbal attacks, like your punches, make incremental inroads on my defenses. "Stop," I say, wrapping my arms around you, an embrace you tolerate for the briefest moment before pushing me away.

"I feel oppressed by your presence," you say, walking out of the room, throwing the remark back at me over your shoulder.

"What are you talking about?" I call back, not wanting the answer, on the edge of knowing it.

You don't return right away, and, when you do, you seem surprised that I'm still on the scene. "I felt this before," you say, "but I couldn't define it exactly. You take up all the air in a room. You have an oppressive presence."

I probably take your remark more literally than I should, but I don't know what else to do with it. "I'm sorry," I say, my regret unfocused.

You wave off my meaningless apology. "Being sorry doesn't change anything. You are who you are."

I resist the self-defeating impulse to defend myself and take a different tack equally humbling. "Just a few weeks ago" I say in a childish squall, "you said that you loved me."

"Really, sweetheart," you say. "One thing doesn't have anything to do with the other."

I wait around in my most nonoppressive mode, waiting for you to recant your disaffection, but it doesn't happen, hasn't happened, has no chance of happening. I am stuck, irrevocably oppressive, oppressing myself and anyone else in the sway of my shadow.

My exit line is not worth thinking about, let alone repeating here.

* * *

A few days later, I receive a phone call from someone calling himself Roger as if the name is supposed to mean something to me, suggesting we meet for a drink the coming Thursday after work.

"I'm busy on Thursday," I say. "Besides, if this is what I think it's about, I don't see the point."

"No point, huh?"

"I think you know what I'm saying," I say.

"Aren't you even a little curious to hear what I have to say? Look it doesn't have to be Thursday. You choose a time and a place and I'll make it my business to be there."

"What about Thursday at four?"

He makes an extended noise, somewhere between a laugh and a groan or some combination thereof. "It's a little early in the day for me, but OK."

"You sure it's OK?" I say.

"Didn't I just say so."

"You sound unconvinced," I say. "How will I know it's you?"

He laughs which breaks up into a cough. "I'll find you, buddy."

*　*　*

At a little after four on Thursday, I make my way to the Brass Bar, a six-block walk from my apartment, after deciding, during a night of fragmentary dreams—one in which I find a translucent baby hiding out in the sock drawer of my dresser—not to bother.

I look around before taking a booth—the place is unchar-acteristically half-empty and ominously silent—but recognize no one who even remotely resembles Roger. None of the all-day topers at the bar return my glance.

I am relieved that Roger isn't here and it suits my sense of irony that, after pushing for this meeting, he is the one not to show up.

A minute or so after I make myself at home in an empty booth—it's almost as if no time has passed—a man about my height and weight, though notably older and without a beard, slides carelessly into the seat across from me.

His arrival thwarts me. In the story I've already written in my head, Roger does not materialize.

Without acknowledging me, he explains his delay. "Something came up at the last minute—I actually had my coat on at the time—one of those crisis-creating, unsolvable problems. I couldn't pull myself away until I did."

There's something familiar and annoying about his manner. "We've met before, I think, haven't we?"

"I recognized you the moment I came in the door, though it doesn't necessarily mean that we've met. I'm sure you know what I mean, no? We may have met but it would have been a long time ago."

An image of a younger Roger—he actually looks like an older version of the baby in my sock drawer—comes to mind. "Didn't we once, maybe four years ago, maybe five, play in a doubles game at the Wall Street Racquet Club?"

"Not likely. I haven't played tennis since I started having problems with my back."

"Lower back? Predominantly on the left side?"

"Right side."

"I remember you had an unorthodox serve that was inexcusably effective."

"Would it were so. My serve, even before my back went out, had been inexcusably ineffective. And it was nothing if not orthodox. I took lessons for almost as many years as I was in analysis. I'm sure you're anxious to know why I asked for this meeting. It wasn't to bounce around my tennis serve."

"I remember now—it was your partner, Cyrus something, he was the one with the odd service motion. It was something like Jacques Tati's serve in *Mr. Hulot's Holiday*."

"The last time I played doubles, I partnered with a man named Sydney."

And then for an almost five-minute stretch—the waiter interrupts whatever it is to take our order—neither of us has anything to say.

It is Roger who eventually breaks the silence. "I have to say you're not at all what I expected." He wags his head at me in reproof.

"How so?"

He shrugs. "For starters, and please don't take this the wrong way, I can't begin to imagine what our mutual friend sees in you. I expected someone better looking with more charisma. No offense."

"Only a little taken."

"Look, I had asked to meet you because I thought—I'm not even sure I'm saying this the right way—that we might make common cause ... Look, it's a dumb idea. I already regret bringing it up."

"The common cause thing, you mean concerning ...?" And I mention your name. "Anyway, I'm out of the picture."

The name, which I'm committed not to divulge in this text, enlists a sigh, perhaps even an accompanying blush. "Yes and no," he says, then he confides with a kind of hollow bravado that he has made up his mind to end his relationship with you.

By this time, people are standing two and three deep at the bar and the booths are filling up, which makes it prohibitively hard to hear someone across from you murmuring, particularly someone like Roger who tends to make conversation as if the listener were an eavesdropper on his introspection.

So I can't vouch for the accuracy of what remains of our conversation. Occasionally your name resounds through the din and the word "love," but not the connecting context. "I have no illusions," I hear him say, a rueful boast. "At my age, what's the point?"

"I hear you," I say, meaning less and more than it suggests.

He leans forward in a confiding posture. "I knew as soon as I saw you that you were someone I could talk to without the usual self-regarding bullshit. I trashed a marriage of sixteen-years duration to be with her. I have a daughter—she'll be graduating Yale at the end of the year—who has never quite forgiven me and whose life is a disaster area because of my divorce from her mother. So you can understand why I have an outsized investment in this relationship and I've hung in like a trooper until now, until last week, when a less obsessional person would have long since cut his losses."

"I've been in situations like …," I start to say, but he interrupts before I can finish the thought.

"On three different occasions I asked { } to marry me. It was in response to my third proposal that she told me there was someone else. The someone else of course was you. I told myself: Roger, don't be an asshole, you'll never get what you want from her, but still I couldn't let go. It was only after I talked to my nutritionist, who serves as an all-purpose advisor, that I found the inner strength to end it."

"Have you told her of your decision?"

"Tonight … Is it true that you're no longer diddling her?"

Maybe he doesn't say diddling—there is wall-to-wall noise in the bar—but it is something like it, meaning approximately the same thing. My impulse is to console him, but I merely nod.

"It would be a nice irony if she lost us both."

I begin to see what you mean by Roger being responsible for the betrayals in his life. His occasional assertiveness is a form of disguise. Something in his manner, something deceptively subtle, asks the casual acquaintance to take advantage of him.

"If neither of us is seeing her," I say, "then her game, if game is the word for it, has been self-defeating. Wouldn't you say?"

"I have to go," he says abruptly, extending his hand as an afterthought.

I do not say that I am pleased to have met him.

We make no arrangements to meet again.

* * *

A month or so after the meeting with Roger, I run into you on the street in front of the Film Forum. At first sighting, I am spectacularly glad to see you. You keep your distance, which disappoints me, act as if you haven't noticed my presence. To protect you, or to protect myself, I also look away.

Then, with a kind of abrupt determination, you come over, calling my name as you approach.

"You're looking the same," you say as if years have passed since we last saw each other. I kiss you awkwardly on the cheek, which you present as if it were the Pope's ring, though in the next moment you wrap your arms around me and give me an extended hug.

"If you're here by yourself," you say, "why don't you join us."

"Us?"

"I'm meeting Roger," you say.

"The endlessly betrayable Roger?"

"What?"

"Not worth repeating," I say. "And how do you know we're even planning to see the same movie?"

"You are here to see the Rohmer," you say, winking at me. "Am I right?"

You are, though to defend myself from your presumptions I am prepared to deny it, when Roger ambles up to us.

"Look who I found," you say.

Roger does not seem pleased at my presence, though he manages a wry, civilized smile, and offers his hand.

It's not that I don't consider going to see the Anthony Mann thriller in the film noir series in the smaller theater. It's just that I end up following the two of you in, which includes entering the same aisle and taking the seat next to yours with Roger on the other side of you. I say end up, though of course no one forces me to follow you into the row you've chosen for us.

When your arm brushes mine, I take my elbow off the arm rest and drop it on my leg like a piece of discarded clothing.

I watch the movie, which is about a married woman taking out a personals ad in order to find a man for her reticent unmarried friend and then meeting with one of the respondents in a succession of dates while pretending to be someone she's not.

You seem to me at the moment like the heroine of the film, a perception I immediately distrust, in certain not easily definable ways.

I can't say who initiates the gesture but we hold hands secretively for a while, your hand withdrawn as the film fades into the titles.

We end up at a café a few blocks from the theater and use the movie to talk in coded ways about the tensions inherent in our immediate situation. Roger, for example, sees the movie as a study in betrayal.

You play us off for the most part with casual even-handedness, though I sense (perhaps mistakenly) that you prefer me to Roger. Once this perception locks in, virtually everything you do provides further evidence for my certainty. At some point, I find myself outraged on Roger's behalf—this is not the you I care about—made uneasy by your casually dismissive treatment of him.

Preferred or not, I am the one that gets up to leave.

"Why don't you come back with us," you say. "I believe I have enough food in the fridge to make dinner for three."

"Thank you for the offer," I say—how grotesquely polite we all are—"but I have other plans. Anyway, I'm sure that Roger, though too civilized to say so, doesn't want me intruding on his date."

"I'd be happy to have you join us," Roger says.

* * *

So. The odd couple plus one trudge over to your apartment, though the sidewalk isn't wide enough to walk three abreast and I find myself, as much by choice as circumstance, pulling up the rear like an orphan.

Once in your apartment, we discover that there is less food in your refrigerator than estimated. The notion that you are prepared to cook a meal for us should have set off an alarm. When I first met you, you used to boast that you never put heat to food unless under duress, though other times you complained wistfully of how you liked the idea of cooking and wished you had more gift for it.

Instead of having dinner, we drink brandy and nibble on hors d'oeuvres left over from an old party—a near rancid tapenade on wheat thins—and watch a French movie about cannibalism in Paris on IFC. Before the bloodshed starts, Roger dozes off on the couch and you mute the sound on the TV and we make conversation in counterpoint to the gory images in hushed voices.

"You're looking very fetching tonight," I say.

"You just want to get laid," you say.

When the movie concludes—there are English subtitles so the lack of sound makes it neither more nor less incoherent—we help Roger into the guest room, take off his shoes and pants and slip him under the cover like a family secret.

I go into the bathroom and throw water on my face, in private unresolved debate on whether to take the subway or not, considering the difficulty in finding a taxi on your street at 1 a.m.

"I'd invite you to share my bed," you say, "but it doesn't seem quite fair, does it, with Roger in the guest room. I'll make up the couch for you."

"I'm thinking of going home."

"That's just silly. You always stay over on Saturday night."

There is something askew in what you say, but I am too unfocused to find the words to define my objection. You throw your arms around me and I take to be an inducement.

"I'm really not overjoyed with the idea of staying on your couch," I hear myself say in a peevish voice hardly recognizable as my own.

"Not overjoyed, huh?" you say. "It was on our second date, if you remember—the night we went to see Mauricio Pollini at Carnegie Hall—that we used the couch to make our own recital. I don't recall any objections that night."

"That was a more innocent time," I say, though I have no recollection of the event you cite. I never went to a Pollini recital with you at Carnegie Hall.

"While you are making your mind up, I'm going to brush my teeth if you have no objections. I believe you know where the sheets are if you want to make up the couch yourself."

I pick up the *Times* crossword puzzle from the foot of the couch while you are in the bathroom—you have completed about a third of it—and scan it with a pen in my hand, resisting an impulse to correct a mistake.

You yank the paper from me when you return, saying you were planning to finish the puzzle yourself for God's sake. I almost grab it back, which is one of the few unexamined impulses I resist that night.

"All right," you say, "you can come into the bedroom if you insist but no sex, OK? I want your word on that."

"No sex," I say.

"You promise?"

"I don't promise."

"OK then."

We have both been drinking steadily for about three hours at that juncture so we have a built-in excuse for irresponsible behavior.

Anyway, I fall asleep as soon as my head hits the pillow, though I am distantly aware of you lying next to me in your satiny purple nightgown, your thigh brushing the back of my hand.

I dream of burrowing my face into some woman's swollen (pregnant?) stomach—she is your sister in the dream, a near twin, someone whose existence you've kept from me—and wake to find myself alone in your bed. After a moment of figuring out where I am, I make my way to the bathroom.

I pee for what seems like five minutes—it's as if I've sprung this endless leak—all the time wondering where you might be. Challenged by your absence, I find my way into the kitchen, which has a small light over the sink, a kind of night-light for dirty dishes. Sure enough there is your scary cat, an oversized, long-haired feral tabby perched on the dishwasher, staring balefully at me, but no sign of you.

I pad back into the bedroom, thinking maybe you have returned in my absence. There are lots of shadows in the dark room, which suggest the possibility of a human form, and I take the trouble to whisper your name, a ghostly call that goes unanswered.

There is only one other place you might be and I refuse to acknowledge the possibility.

I put on my pants—I had been sleeping in my underwear—and sit hunkered over on the edge of the bed, wondering if I have it in me to get back to sleep. I close my eyes and imagine you standing over me, your fingers brushing my lips.

When I hear a murmur of voices—it may be from the apartment upstairs or the loose wiring in my head—I leave the room again to check out their source.

At that moment, the door to the guest room opens mysteriously and a shadowy figure emerges from the darkness. You are wearing a flimsy pale green robe over your satin nightgown.

"What's going on?" you ask me.

"I might have asked the same question," I say.

"I was just checking to see if Roger was all right," you say.

"Was he?"

"Oh yes."

"No surprise there."

"Don't be ugly, sweetie," you say. "I spent most of the night in bed with you, didn't I?"

"Did you? I don't remember much of what went on."

"You were asleep," you whisper. "You slept like a stone."

"Oh," I say. "That must explain it."

"Are you being sarcastic, sweetie?" you ask. "I'm not responsible for you being asleep, am I? I'm going to make a pot of coffee if the interrogation is over."

The interrogation, as you call it, isn't over, but you don't wait for my permission to leave. "Wait a second," I say to your back or imagine myself saying.

In the bathroom, I am assaulted by the weary, unsympathetic image that peers back from the mirror. The toothbrush I use when I stay over is not in its usual place and, after looking through the medicine cabinet to no avail, I brush my teeth with my finger. As I leave the bathroom, Roger, who is standing outside the door awaiting his turn, insists on shaking my hand.

I have to get out of there immediately, I tell myself, working up a sense of urgency some part of me continues to resist.

No matter, I stay for breakfast—you have made blueberry pancakes with sausage and grits on the side. The temptation of the pancakes gets the better of my internal alarm.

I end up sitting directly across from Roger with you at the head of the table. "What do you guys want to do today?" you ask.

I know I have something else on for today, though I can't remember—it seems symptomatic of a larger failure—what that something else might be.

"Sorry," I say, getting up. "I have other plans."

"Really?" you say. "What are these other plans?"

I wave off your presumptuous question. "Something I set up awhile back."

"Well, if you can't come up with a better excuse than that," you say, "I don't see why we should let you off."

Roger guffaws with his mouth full of food—blueberries no doubt, but it looks like he's spitting blood—catching the spray by rushing his napkin to his face.

"You know what I'd like to do," Roger says. "I'd like to see the Pollock show at the Modern. I've seen it once but I think a second visit will more than repay itself."

"The Modern tends to have long lines on Sunday," you say, "and I know our friend here hates crowds."

"Your friend here has a previous appointment," I say.

"Absolutely," you say. "How could I have forgotten? I just thought, not important really, that it would be nice for the three of us to do something together."

Nice!? I have no idea what's going on with you. In any event, I am making my way to the door.

I glance back at Roger while you are doing your number and he seems to be smiling bravely, unaware that his face can be read, through barely endurable pain.

* * *

I come home to my lonely apartment after spending the long escapeless day, parading through museums so crowded that someone's head has morphed into almost every artwork.

* * *

The following e-mail arrives Monday morning.

> Wasn't Sunday an extraordinary day!
> We must all do it again soon.
> Roger
> His note makes me want to put my fist through the wall, though I can't (or won't) say exactly why.

* * *

Two weeks later when you call to invite me to dinner for "just the two of us," I have to ask you to repeat your invitation before I can wrap my mind around it.

"Gee, I hope you're not mad at me," you say. "You know appearances are not always what they seem. You just need to have more trust in people."

"I trust appearances," I say.

"Please don't be clever at my expense, OK? If you don't want to come to dinner, just say so. I'm not going to fall apart."

I have already fallen apart, but it isn't anything I care to admit to you so I stall for time, hoping to intuit which of my choices, once irrevocably made, would be the less regrettable. "I may have a prior appointment," I say. "I'll have to look in my book."

"So you won't come—is that what you're telling me?"

"I'll see if I can get out of it and call you back," I say.

"I don't want to be the cause of someone else's disappointment," you say. "We'll do it another time."

"The appointment was made so long ago," I say, "I'm not sure if it's still in place."

"It doesn't matter."

"I'll call you back within two hours," I say.

"If you do, you do. I won't hold my breath."

My first impulse after I hang up is to call back (after a suitable delay) and accept your invitation, though some whisper of dignity rises in me to refuse.

To escape a decision I seem unable to make, I go out for a walk in the night air, end up at the Brass Bar, linger over two beers, trade quips with the bartender who is an aspiring stand-up comic, and faze out on a hockey game on TV as if I were watching a series of fast moving abstractions reconfigure themselves.

An hour and twenty minutes pass and I become increasing obsessed with the arbitrary two hour deadline I have given you for my decision.

Although I might have called you from the bar, I rush home. A half block from my apartment, I see you, or think I do, hurrying toward me.

This makes everything all right until I discover it is someone else, a different shadow. The stranger, an Asian woman who may or may not be a streetwalker, asks me for a cigarette and for a moment I imagine myself going off with her and we end up dancing together in her one-room apartment, the wall space covered by posters from *The Wizard of Oz.*

"Sorry, I don't smoke," I say.

"I usually don't make that mistake," she says.

When I get inside my own place and remove my jacket, leaving it on the chair near the phone, it is five minutes short of the two hour deadline. By the time I dial your number and, in doing so, revise my decision yet again, two more minutes have passed.

I get a busy signal then wait thirty seconds and push redial. The same message repeats itself.

Again: busy.

Your circumstantial unavailability fuels a self-induced anxiety.

I can imagine you saying, "I held the invitation two hours for you, which you asked for, right? But your time has elapsed and so I made other plans."

Anyway, I dial your number again, not trusting the redial to do its job, and this time it rings. I know you are there because only five minutes ago, the line was busy, but the phone keeps ringing without event—at least seven times to my hasty count—and then your recorded message breaks the pattern.

And then, as I am about to say that I am free to come to dinner, that I am looking forward to seeing you, the phone goes dead. What is that about?

I dial again, assuming that you were momentarily indisposed, assuming whatever I can to justify the unlikely, and I get another busy signal. In childish pique (see, I do not disguise my shortcomings), I hurl the phone across the room, watch it land unharmed on the couch.

I have small—very small—tolerance for frustration and, though alone (unseen except by the reader), I am nevertheless embarrassed by my behavior.

One more try, I tell myself. and that's it. This is my last call.

On the third (or fourth) ring, a man answers (it may even be a wrong number) and I hang up without speaking in a blind rage that takes a long time, months perhaps, even years to resolve.

FIVE

The next time we meet is in another country—Paris, as a matter of fact, the city of love (or is it light?)—at my brother's wedding to your half-sister. In the intervening three years, during which I publish my third book (a modestly reviewed meditation on war called *The Lion's Share*) I think of you no more than five or six times. From the moment I discover you, I try to catch your eye, but you never turn in my direction, seem occupied by the details of the ceremony or perhaps preoccupied in private reverie.

At the reception that follows, one thing or another keeps me from approaching you, an ongoing intention unobtrusively thwarted. I have the sense on no evidence beyond the fact that circumstance never brings you close to my side that you're willfully avoiding me.

I am the only one of my brother's family present for the occasion and, from what I can make out, one of the few Americans at hand. You are there with several people, perhaps one of them your husband, and appear to be an intimate of the bride. It is only later that I discover that there is a family connection as well—you share, or so everyone says, the same absent father.

For a moment, I catch your eye and wav and you make an ambiguous face at me in return, mocking, petulant, self-parodying, impossible to decipher.

I begin to wonder if it is really you and not some uncanny lookalike when the bride's mother sidles up to me and asks if I would be so kind—the request elaborate and, under the circumstances, unrefusable. She is asking me to dance with her.

It is not what I want to do and I make an awkward excuse or two (bad hip, naturally clumsy), which she steadfastly ignores, before leading her on to the floor.

"My name is Madeleine," she says in barely accented English. "I want to hear much about you. Are you a true person like your frére?"

What can I say? Whatever I come up with is bound to seem either boastful or self-deprecating or some embarrassing combination of the two. "The question that had been on my mind," I say, the first of several mistakes I make that evening, "is whether the mother is as beautiful as the daughter and that is already answered before I ask it."

"*Je ne comprends,*" you say. "I am or I am not?"

"You are of course," I say.

"Oo la la," you say. "Certainly not. It is a cruel compliment because so patently false and insincere." All this is said as if she meant something else—not easy to say what that else might be—altogether. We finish the dance in relative silence, and I have the sense that I have disappointed Madeleine's expectations.

"*Merci, monsieur,*" Madeleine says when the music has stopped. "Thank you, Donald's brother, for indulging the whim of an older woman."

"My pleasure," I say and Madeleine laughs as if we shared some private joke, and waltzes off, aware of an audience, to greet whomever's next on her agenda.

I spot you at one of the hors d'oeuvres tables and I come up on you from behind and wait with willed patience for you to acknowledge me.

"Not here," you say without turning around. "Later."

"When?" I ask.

"Go away," you say, and I do.

* * *

It comes out while I am paying my respects to the married couple that the bride is your half-sister on your father's side and that the two of you have become fast friends on short acquaintance.

"I'm sorry your dad couldn't join us," the bride says.

"He's also sorry," I say to which my brother, standing behind the bride, rolls his eyes.

The reason our father is not at the wedding is because my brother is not speaking to him, but apparently that is not the story in circulation.

Madeleine appears and asks me if I need a place to stay for the night and I have trouble remembering if other arrangements were made and I say I don't know.

"Of course you'll stay with us," Madeleine says. "I'm not sure who else I've committed to, but we'll find out soon enough."

Dinner comes first and I drift off with what appears to be an insider group which includes Donald and his bride, Madeleine and her fourth husband, Bruno, and you and your date among others. You still have not quite acknowledged me.

During dinner at trendy Soixante-neuf, it strikes me that I left my overnight case in the closet of the reception hall or perhaps in the trunk of a taxi en route to the restaurant. My anxiety at its loss slips away after my second glass of wine.

Just as the dessert course arrives, as if it were their cue, Donald and Lola slip off on their honeymoon. When they are gone, Madeleine, who is at the head of the table, gives an audible sigh of relief.

Then I find myself sitting on a jump seat in an overcrowded taxi with Madeleine and Bruno, you and your date (whose name

I understand is Roget) traveling to Madeleine's house in the thirteenth *arrondisement*.

When we arrive, there are some other wedding guests waiting at the door to whom Madeleine has also promised lodging for the night. We congregate in the living room to wait for our assignments.

A mathematical problem ensues. There are four guest bedrooms in Madeleine's charming, somewhat cluttered house, and nine people to accommodate.

It makes sense of course to award the bedrooms to the couples, which leaves me, the only single on the scene, odd man out.

"I have a perfectly comfortable folding cot," Madeleine says, first in French then in English. "The question is, where do we locate this cot?"

"I appreciate your concern," I say, "but it's no problem for me to stay at a hotel."

"I will take it as an insult if you leave," she says, " and I am not one, I promise you, quick to forgive."

To avoid seeming difficult, I offer to spend the night on the living room couch.

"I wouldn't think of it," Madeleine says. "Not at all. I will put a screen between us to give you intimacy. You will stay in my room."

"I think you mean privacy," I say.

"Do I?" Madeleine says. "Of course."

Everyone by this time has gone off to their assigned rooms except you and your date. During the preceding conversation, you have been browsing through the bookshelves that line the walls with the kind of concentration that seems to shut everything out so I am taken aback when you turn and say, "As always, Madeleine, you are too kind for your own good. This is your house and you have a right to be comfortable in it. So let me make a counter suggestion."

"Such as?" Madeleine says, perplexed as we all are by your unexpected intervention.

"We can just as easily install your lovely screen in the room Roget and I will be staying in," you say.

"I wouldn't hear of it," Madeleine says. "The matter is settled."

"Really, Madeleine," you say, "it makes no one happy to have you martyr yourself. Roget and I would be pleased to share our room in your lovely house with Donald's brother."

The debate between the two women goes on for longer than needs to be described and I watch like a spectator with only a marginal rooting interest in the outcome.

I am uncomfortably aware, though I have no idea of the history behind it, that the two of you have no love for one another.

At some point, Roget comes over to you, puts his hand on your arm and says in French—the following an estimate of his remarks— "This is Madeleine's house, dear, and the decision where a guest will be put up should be hers to make." He says this in a quiet voice but you push him away and whisper what I imagine to be the French equivalent of fuck off.

Roget turns to me and shrugs.

"Oo la la," Madeleine says. And then, turning in my direction, adds, "You decide please."

The narrow-eyed stare she gives me has a different message altogether. It is as if she is daring me to refuse her and if I dare, I fall beyond the pale of her forebearance. She will not, perhaps never, forgive me.

"Whatever you decide is fine," I say, trying to occupy an ephemeral middle ground that probably does not exist.

"Then it is decided," Madeleine says, "I'll get the cot for you and some linen." She sweeps out of the room in modest triumph.

Roget seems relieved, but you ask him, virtually order him, to go to the kitchen and get you a glass of white wine.

He hesitates before leaving, seems troubled, considers refusing you, but decides to postpone whatever scene he will eventually make.

And then for the first time that evening, we are alone. Everyone else has left the stage.

"Look," you say, "this has nothing to do with us; I want you to understand that. You and I are through as we both know; this had to do with Madeleine."

"Yes?"

"Yes. Madeleine has a sweet tooth for younger men. She is a notorious man-eater. I stood up to her to protect you from an embarrassing situation."

"I don't see why you think I need protecting," I say. "Besides, Bruno will be in the room, won't he?"

You shake your head, impatient with what seems to you my willed innocence. "They have separate rooms," you say, not looking at me, watching the door for Madeleine's return. "Don't you see what's going on? Are you so totally oblivious?"

Unwilling to understand the intensity of your concern, I nevertheless thank you for your trouble on my behalf just as Madeleine returns.

"Your bed is made up," Madeleine says, making a point of saying *bonne nuit* to your back as you leave.

Madeleine's room is not as large as I imagined it, but there is a six foot high Japanese-style screen between her plush queen-size bed (which she makes a point of showing me) and my austere single. A well-appointed private bathroom, which includes a bidet and double sinks with gleaming faucets, is on my side of the room.

I wait a few minutes to let Madeleine use the bathroom, but when she doesn't appear after about ten minutes I take my turn, following my usual routine except for the addition of a mild sleeping pill, and get into my cot, which is reassuringly comfortable. Your warning makes a brief appearance in my thoughts. Before I know it, before I can obsess about the difficulty I have falling asleep in other people's beds, I have fallen asleep.

I have fallen asleep.

I have fallen asleep.

The third of my dreams has to do with rescuing a woman in some historical movie (of indeterminate period) who I discover tied to a tree in the Bois de Boulogne. "Only a man pure of art has the power to free me," she says.

And yet I have been the one chosen to untie her. Is it possible that I have been mistaken for someone else and so arbitrarily put into a false role? I look for a sharp-edged stone to cut her bonds.

The woman, who is dressed in tatters, laughs mockingly at my efforts. "If you are the right person, all you have to do is kiss the hem of my robe and my ropes will untie of their own accord."

I hesitate. Which of the tatters represents her robe, I wonder. "And what will happen if I am the wrong person?"

"We will both die," she says. "I hope you understand that I am speaking metaphorically."

How can I determine whether I am sufficiently pure of art, whatever that means. A kind of inertia or paralysis holds me as I try to assess the potential negative consequences of the good deed I am asked to perform—like what is a metaphorical death?—when I hear footsteps.

"What the hell's holding you back?" the woman says, then adds something in a language that is not one of mine.

Is it possible to be aware of dreaming or is that an inherent contradiction? I find, unexpectedly, a Swiss Army knife in my right hand pocket and I use the first blade to release, which turns out to be a bottle opener, to cut the woman's bonds, spilling the smallest possible amount of blood.

She rubs her wrists, then puts her arms around my neck and mumbles in a grudging tone of voice something about being forever in my debt. "You have a kiss coming," she says. "Where would you like it?"

I am embarrassed to say what I want, and she laughs and says, "All right, dummy, then I'll make the choice for you." The next thing I know we are on the mossy ground together, rolling around, struggling for position.

It is at this point I usually awake, but tonight the dream insists on playing itself out.

When I open my eyes at first light, I am shivering and sweating, my covers in a sprawl on the floor next to the cot.

I drag myself up to go to the bathroom, but the door is latched from the inside so I return to my cot. Exhausted, I try to go back to sleep—that is, I shut my eyes—but the urgencies of my bladder become the more crucial concern.

So I put on the gray suit I wore at the wedding—my overnight case lost—and go off to find an unoccupied bathroom. The first two I try are, like my own, latched from within and I begin to consider other alternatives.

Then I remember there being a closet with a toilet in it right off the kitchen and I work my way down two flights of stairs. In the dark, nothing seems quite like it was in the light. Somehow I manage to find myself inside the closetlike enclosure. With the door closed and latched against my back, there is barely room to stand.

After peeing, I rub my hands against the sides of my pants, then comb my hair with my fingers. When I step out of the bathroom after a serious struggle with the latch, the light is on in the kitchen and Roget in his overcoat is sitting with his back to me, drinking coffee from a mug the size of a soup bowl.

Looking over his shoulder to take my measure, he offers me a scornful smile.

"Bonjour," I say.

"*Ça va,*" he says in return.

The amenities out of the way, he finishes his coffee in silence.

The coffeepot is one of those plunger types I have no idea how to use but I stumble around self-consciously opening cupboards. "Where does she keep the coffee?" I ask him.

Roget seems not to hear me or perhaps not to understand the question.

He is washing his coffee cup when you come into the kitchen and say something to him in French—the inflection suggests a question—which he answers, or seems to, without turning to look at you.

Roget pushes open the side door, the door that comes off the kitchen, makes no attempt to button his coat, and disappears from the scene.

You walk to the window and look out after him, tracking his progress, or so it seems.

"What was that about?" I ask.

You ignore my question, retreat to the table in a defeated posture, slump into the chair farthest from mine.

"Are you all right?" I ask.

"No."

"Is there something I can do for you?"

"Absolutely not." You keep your face turned away.

I take sips of my coffee and wait my turn, my patience running thin as the coffee turns cold. After a while, after my cup is drained, I get up and announce that I am going back to my room.

"Don't you leave me too," you say.

"Did Roget leave you?" I ask. "The impression he gave me is that you asked him to go."

You raise your head momentarily. "Is that what he told you? Whatever, it comes to the same thing, doesn't it? The fact is, he's gone."

I sit down at the table, honoring your request, leaving an empty seat between us. After a moment, you take the seat next to me and put your head on my shoulder. And then I put my arm around you—where else can it go?—and your body stiffens almost imperceptibly.

And that's the way we are, trapped by the flashbulb of the imaginary onlooker's imaginary camera, when Madeleine discovers us, sitting cheek to shoulder at the kitchen table.

She makes a point of not looking directly at us, asks the room if anyone—we are the only two in the kitchen—would like some breakfast. She has, I notice, put her long gray hair in an over-elaborate bun, a designer chopstick seemingly holding it in place.

"I almost never eat breakfast," I say.

You seem about to speak, but instead get up from the table, nod to me, and leave the room.

"She knows I didn't want her here," Madeleine says. "It's no trouble, you know, for me to make something for you. I'm one of those women who enjoys to challenge the kitchen. And so what are your plans for today? What would you like to do with your day?"

I have no plans, which is to say I had planned to return home as soon as it seemed appropriate to leave. At the same time, I have a kind of anxious unobjectified foreboding. I want desperately to get out of the kitchen, but I am unable to come up with an acceptable excuse to take off.

"Before you go," Madeleine says, "there's something I feel I should say. If you knew me better you would know this is not my style to criticize, but somebody, some friend should tell you this for your own good. I say this very reluctantly because I believe there is some good in her too. I suppose there is good in everybody, but who knows."

Then she goes on to tell me this extraordinary story about you, insisting on her reluctance to give out this information while of course giving it out in profusion. According to Madeleine, there is an unsolved mystery in your past, a former husband who died suddenly under, as she puts it, a dark cloud. Though nothing was ever proved, there were those who thought that you had arranged his murder, or possibly even committed the murder yourself.

"I for one don't believe she's capable of murder," Madeleine said, "no more than any of us, though for an American she's extremely subtle. In any event, I like you too much not to let you know what you might be facing. I know with my own eyes that you are sweet on her so don't deny it."

*   *   *

Later in the day, when you drive me to the airport, you ask in a casual voice if I had sex with Madeleine when I spent the night in her room.

I don't see that it is any of your business, which is what I don't say or at least don't say aloud. Instead I ask if it's true that you had been married and widowed since the last time we ran into one another.

"Well, did you or didn't you?" you say.

"Why do you care?" I ask.

"That means you did, doesn't it? What a helpless innocent you are. Frankly, I'm embarrassed on your behalf."

My suspicion is that the woman in the dream was Madeleine and that what happened between us extended beyond the dream. Nothing is certain, however. "You were married before or you weren't, which is it?" I ask.

We drive another twenty minutes in silence when I realize the road we are on is not going to Orly and ask, as anyone might in my position, for an explanation.

"I was wondering when you'd notice," you say. "There's a totally charming cabin in Provence, isolated from virtually everything, that I've been invited to use. I was in no mood to go alone so I thought I'd kidnap you if you have no objections."

I look at my watch. My flight to JFK leaves Orly in an hour and fifteen minutes. "How far are we from the airport?" I ask.

"Too far to walk," you say. "Look, I promise you it will be different this time. If you prefer to go to the US by yourself to going to Provence with me, I'll drive you to Orly. Deal? Either way, you have to tell me you didn't sleep with my sister's mother."

"I didn't sleep with my sister's mother, I mean your sister's mother," I say.

"I don't know whether to believe you," you say. "Can I believe you? How can I? Do I even want to believe you? Do you even care whether I believe you or not?"

"I'd appreciate it if you'd take me to the airport," I say, a gesture at reclaiming some pretense of dignity.

You pull over onto the apron and stop the car with a jolting screech. I expect you to ask me to get out of the car, which I plan to refuse, but instead you stare (or look blindly) ahead as if your image were paused, and say nothing for more time than I know what to do with.

When I look at my watch you unfreeze long enough to glance in my direction. "It's disgusting to always want to know the time," you say. "If you live in the moment, you have no need of a watch."

It may be true that I almost never live in the moment, though I have always aspired to make the necessary adjustment. On the other hand, living in the moment does you no particular good when you have a flight to make.

A police car pulls off the highway and stops about fifty feet behind us. A few minutes pass—it seems like no time at all—but no one emerges from the vehicle.

"There's some dope in the glove compartment," you say. "When they stop you in France, they tend to search the car. I don't know what will catch his attention more, rushing off or staying put."

"We're probably better off returning to the highway," I say.

"You think?"

"We're less conspicuous as part of the general traffic, don't you think?"

"You make the decision."

"Let's go," I say and we pull back onto the highway, sliding in front of a paper goods truck that honks its horn at us.

"Even when I was with others," you say, "it's always been you."

After a moment, I turn around to see if there's anything to concern us coming up from behind.

* * *

Years later, when we meet at a party given by people neither of us have met before, we go off together into the coatroom, which is also the master bedroom, and endeavor to catch up. At some point the discussion turns to the confusing events of our brief time together in San Remy.

"It was kind of you to come with me," you say. "I'm sorry I behaved like such a bitch. Look, I never wanted it to happen the way it did, but—I have to say it—you got on my nerves."

"Did I?"

"It was all my fault I'm sure," you say. "It was a difficult time for me as you know. A man I was crazy about, a man totally undeserving, dumped me." We are sitting on the coats a foot or so apart and you offer me your hand.

"I thought I was the one that owed you an apology," I say.

"You were always so nice to me," you say. "Really, you were too nice—that was your problem. I've always had trouble getting on with men who were nice to me."

I have trouble reconciling the image of niceness with the sense of myself I carry away from that strange period in my life. "I behaved unconscionably in San Remy," I insist.

"Not at all," you say. "I understand perfectly why you felt the need to get away."

"I should at least have left a note, some kind of explanation," I say.

"The fact of your absence was explanation enough. You realized I was putting minute doses of poison in your food. I understood that. Why wouldn't you run away? I just wonder you had enough strength to walk by yourself to the next town."

"I left you the car because I was sort of hoping you'd come after me," I say.

You retrieve your hand and use it along with the other to cover your face. "I can't believe you wanted me to come after you. Why would you? Why would you possibly?"

For a moment I let the conversation die, feeling with some desperation the need to get away, the need to escape further explanation. When I fled the cabin in San Remy, as I recall, I had been feeling a little weak in the legs, a light sweat on my forehead, my stomach in minor turmoil. All pretense. The illness was just a ruse on my part to throw you off—I didn't want to have to explain my need to be on my own. I had so thoroughly internalized my sense of being desperately ill, my body accepted the implications as though they were real. I even collapsed a few times while running.

"I just wanted to see how far I could take it," you say, your hands still over your face. "You may not want to believe this, but I never intended to go all the way. I want you to believe that. I really do."

I get up from the bed, leaving my coat somewhere in the pile, and edging my way through the crowd, nodding to the woman I had exchanged smiles with earlier in the evening, exit the party, summon the elevator and, without waiting for its arrival, scramble down nine flights to the lobby and then into the street, crossing my arms in front of me as a stay against the shock of the night air.

For the first block or so, I walk briskly, but then as I near the subway, I slow down as if all this desperate hurrying had tired me out. In fact, I avoid going into the subway and continue to walk downtown perhaps to the next stop, which is eighteen blocks away, the streets quiet, almost deserted at this time of night. The moon in a crescent phase misted over, offering a suspicion of light as if coming from behind a closed door.

I must have walked fifteen blocks in all when I glance behind me for the first time and see, or imagine I see, some incalculable distance away, a shadow figure running toward me, holding up something, some offering, a coat perhaps or some kind of oddly shaped weapon. Deciphering my perception costs me no more than a moment or two. And then of course I pick up my stride, continue on my way, my urgency unabated, but like in a dream I suddenly feel the poison flash through my veins, the microscopic doses retarding my progress in imperceptible ways and I sense that before long, before I reach the entrance to the next station of the subway—this is a recurrent unfinished scenario—I will be caught by whomever it is coming up behind me (it is always you) prepared to accept whatever comes next.

SIX

I remember a time (in a dream perhaps) when we ran toward each other on a crowded city street and came together—we were mocking the conventions of a certain kind of romantic film—in a rather cautious, disappointing hug. You insist it never happened, though the memory remains remarkably vivid.

"If I met you again after years of not seeing you, it would be the same between us as it is now," you say. "People don't change. Even as I get older to others, to myself I always remain the same."

It is possible that I'm putting words in your mouth.

You had asked me to meet you at the Brass Bar, a place we used to hang out at when we both drank to tell me something you couldn't or wouldn't relay over the phone.

The mystery of your news has piqued my curiosity to the point that I've already imagined three possible alternate scenarios.

In scenario one you tell me that you've decided to move in with our mutual friend, Roger, and you wanted me to hear it from you first. It is a trial arrangement, you say, hardly permanent, but you both hope (and why wouldn't you?) that it will be a successful trial.

And that you'd like to have my blessings to accompany you on this precipitous and somewhat frightening step.

In scenario two you tell me that you have just learned that you are, as all the signs indicated, pregnant and you would appreciate it greatly if I would accompany you to an abortion clinic as moral support. I do not ask whose child it might be and you do not volunteer the information. I do not have to be a mathematician to know that it is not mine.

In scenario three, you tell me that you woke up this morning with the inescapable sense that it was possible that you were in love with me and had been avoiding my company for the past several months as a form of denial. You were eager, anxious even, to get my response to your news in person so you would have a better sense of how to proceed.

"I don't know what to say," I say.

"I don't know what to say."

"Do you want the polite answer or the one I'll regret afterward?"

"I can understand," you say, "how this might be difficult for you to accept. It's not my intention to hurt you. It's never been my intention to hurt you. I just want us, the three of us, if at all possible, to remain friends."

"I asked you because I didn't know who else to ask. I think you understand what I'm saying."

"I can understand your distrust. I distrust myself as much as you distrust me. Still, I hope I'm being sincere."

I reject the first several invitations to come to dinner before yielding to your relentless campaign to keep me in the picture. Even so, I arrive forty minutes late, which I know without being told is a form of hostility. To cover my tracks, I bring over an expensive bottle of wine, a young Medoc not quite ready to drink.

After you go into the operating room—we have nothing or too much to say to each other on the way over, which is the same thing—the receptionist asks me if "your wife" had anything to eat in the past three hours or so. Since I've only been with you for the past thirty-five minutes, it is not a question I am equipped to answer. "What would happen if she had eaten within three hours?" I ask. "You never know," the receptionist says. "It could be dangerous." "Won't the doctor ask her?" "That's my job," she says. "I'm supposed to check that out before I let them in to see the doctor. In your wife's case I don't know what I was thinking, but I let her get by without asking the question."

As it turns out, I'm not the only one invited to dinner. There is another couple, who I meet at the door going in, and a single woman, Roger's much younger half-sister, who (I believe, unless I have that wrong) has just come over from England and is staying with the two of you until she can find a place of her own. I hand Roger the bottle of wine I've brought, for which he thanks me effusively while glancing disparagingly at the label. "I know next to nothing about continental wines," he says.

You make a show of being disappointed (perhaps that's unfair on my part) at my muted reaction to your news, and after that to your superfluous avowal of sincerity. I'm not sure what you expected. Was I supposed to leap in the air with unbridled delight. "What brought about this discovery?" I ask.

On my left at table is the unattached woman, Elizabeth, and on my right is the female half of the other couple whose name— something starting with an F—I never quite get. Elizabeth tends to silence except to answer questions, and even then offers no more than a few words, words painstakingly chosen to avoid so much as a hint of intimate revelation. On the other hand, F has a lot to say, much of it the most banal form of chatter.

"You can't go in there," the receptionist says, but I do. It is like the primal dream of walking into your parents' bedroom and discovering them in the sexual act.

You have made an uncharacteristically elaborate meal and we are into the third or fourth course, which consists of a pork chop nesting in an apple-cranberry puree, when Elizabeth makes her first unsolicited remarks. "You don't like my brother much, do you?" she says.

My off-limits presence causes a collective hypersonic groan, the dust forming skeletal exclamation points on the white walls. You are the only one to speak words. "Get out of here," you say. "When did you eat last?" I ask. "Please leave," you say. "Can't you see you're not wanted here." "It's dangerous unless more than three hours have elapsed," I say. "Please," you say. "We'll talk about this later."

I had no sense of Elizabeth's presence—I couldn't even have described her if somebody had blindfolded me on the spot—until she makes the accusation concerning her brother in this small childlike voice, every word enunciated with equal stress. That's when I turn to take her in, confronted by the fierce intelligence in her face. I had been planning to deny her assertion, but I can see immediately the pointlessness of lying to her. "It has nothing to do with your brother," I say.

Elizabeth returns her attention to her food. I notice that you are watching us with this troubled look on your face. "There's a little piece of heaven on my plate," F announces to no one in particular.

It's not that I think you're being insincere—well it is and it isn't—or not that so much as that your so-called revelation could easily be rescinded tomorrow or the day after that or even in the next hour by an opposing self-discovery. "Of course I'm pleased to hear it," I say in this grim voice that causes you to laugh. "When I look at you now," you say, "I begin to wonder who I thought I was thinking of when I told myself I loved you."

"It's all right," Elizabeth whispers, "I don't much like him either." When I laugh nervously at Elizabeth's remark, I catch you glaring at me. F says, turning away from Roger with whom she'd been discussing some movie neither of them had seen, "I'm just wild for the taste of dill. If it were up to me, it would be included in every dish. Do you know what I mean?" I nod, or don't, trying to remember (did I ever know?) what signifies the taste of dill. "Then why are you staying in their house?" I ask Elizabeth.

The doctor holds his scalpel, or whatever instrument it is, poised in the air as if it were a conductor's baton, as I back out the door. "Sorry, I interrupted," I say. "I was worried." "Everything's under control," the nurse says, holding a hypodermic needle behind her back.

A waitress comes by and we each order the house pale ale. "This was not an easy confession to make," you say between sips. "And I have to say you've not made it any easier. What do you want to do?" "What do you want to do?" I ask. "Where do you want to take this?" "Since you ask, sweetheart, there's a movie starting at 7:40 at the Angelica that I'd like to catch."

A half hour later you emerge from the operating room, huddled over, the nurse a half-step behind you. "Would you like a wheelchair?" she asks you. You shake your head in this weary way, but then the nurse asks the question again. I get up from my molded plastic chair and meet you halfway, offering you a hand which you refuse.

Roger holds up his wineglass and takes a sip before offering a toast: "To a joyous occasion made all the more joyous by having good friends around to share it with." Oddly, no one else raises a glass except the man who is with F and whose name is either Heinz or Hans or something else altogether different. You pour yourself a glass of seltzer and, after looking around the table at the non-participating guests, join the toast. Eventually F follows suit, leaving only Roger's sister and the narrator of our story with our glasses conspicuously not uplifted. "Well, you two," Roger says. "To the chef," I say, lifting my glass. "To the chef," Roger echoes and we sip from our glasses with relative synchronicity. "Traitor," Elizabeth whispers or perhaps I imagine it, not bothering to look in her direction until the toast is put to rest.

I come around to your side of the car to help you out. "Don't bother," you say, but you teeter when you walk so I accompany you in the elevator to your apartment, which is on the ninth floor. You unlock the door and I help you in, my arm around your waist, and you say, "Thank you, but I really don't need your help; I really don't." I stand around awkwardly, watching you bounce off the door as you lurch into the bedroom. "Are you sure you're going to be all right?" I ask and get no answer. I pace the living room, consider going home, but end up sitting down in your not-quite-comfortable easy chair.

After the meat course, there is a second salad course—a puff of unidentifiable greens (perhaps arugula) circled by tangerine slices—and Roger makes a joke about no one being able to get up from the table after the dinner is finished to which you take exception. "I just wanted to do something elegant," you say, "something in the grand manner. This is the menu, or as close to it as I could get with local provisions, that a wife of one of the Russian tsars made for her husband before she had him killed. I'm sorry if it doesn't meet with your approval."

"Nothing would make me happier," you say, "than to see you genuinely happy, but that's always been out of my hands. You've heard what I have to say so what do you have to say?" I suggest a walk, which invites a skeptical look, and signal to the wrong waitress for our bill, which comes in any event from another direction.

I wake, slumped back in a chair in your living room, unaware of how I got there, when I'm suddenly aware of you crossing the room in slow motion, your backless slippers slapping the floor. "I'm still bleeding," I hear you say. "Shouldn't the bleeding have stopped by now?" "What did the doctor say?" I hear myself answer. "Would I have asked you if I knew?" you say, disappearing from the room.

There is a police action outside the restaurant, five uniformed cops surrounding a homeless Asian man of about sixty, who is waving his arms and talking to himself. One of the cops has his gun drawn. A small crowd looks on as if they were deer caught in some universal headlight. I try to move you in an opposite direction, but you refuse to relinquish your vigil. "Shouldn't we do something?" you say.

Roger sulks as the dessert course circulates and you pretend not to notice. "Do you give doggy bags," F asks, "for those who can't finish this wonderful meal?" Hans, on the other hand, finishes his lemon mousse bomb in short order and reaches across the table to annex F's. "It's scrumptious," F says, yielding her dish—the dessert itself untouched—with apparent relief. Elizabeth offers me hers, but in fact I've only been able to get down a third of mine. Roger, after only a few bites, rushes off to the bathroom, his hand on his stomach. You survey the table, shaking your head in my direction, with an amused smile on your face. "I have to say," you say, "that Hans is the only one that gets an 'A'."

You approach the policeman next to the one who has his gun drawn and ask what danger the man they've surrounded represents. I can't hear the rest of the conversation, but there are several exchanges back and forth before you return to my side. "What happened?" I ask. At first you don't answer, but instead take my arm and urge me away down the street in the direction I originally offered. I have to ask again to get my answer and still you hesitate as if we were dealing here with classified information. "He threatened to arrest me for obstructing justice," you say, looking over your shoulder. I am tempted to laugh but I can see that you are in no mood to be amused by absurdity.

You ask me to help you lift something when the others go into the living room with their espresso cups, but that is only a ruse so that you can ask me something else. "If you think I'm making a big mistake, I wish you'd tell me," you say. "I think you're making a big mistake," I say. "You don't really," you say, "do you? Or is that the voice of jealousy talking?" That's when Roger enters the kitchen and sees us with our heads together and I can tell from his scowl that he has put the worst possible interpretation on our being together. "How are you feeling, darling?" you say to him. "Is there anything I can do for you?"

There seem to be police cars everywhere, the next street blocked off, and we walk determinedly in silence as if no dialogue is possible between us until we're outside the law's ubiquitous presence. "It's an illusion, isn't it?" you say. "It's the plot of a bad movie when a man and a woman who have been friends the way we have suddenly decide they love each other. Of course they love each other. That's what friendship's about, isn't it? Friends love one another." We are standing on a corner having this talk when a police car drives by and the cop not driving waves to us to move on.

"You used a milk product in the dessert without telling me" Roger says in a voice that alternates between fret and accusation. "You know I'm lactose intolerant." "I guess I knew that but it slipped my mind," you say. "Forgive me?" "How can I not?" he says. I am standing behind them in an awkward spot and I have to work my way between them to get by. "You're such a sweet man," she says. They have their arms around each other as I clatter out of the room, temporarily invisible by general consent.

"You don't have to stay," you say returning to the bedroom after an extended imprisonment in the bathroom with the door conspicuously latched from inside. "Don't think I don't appreciate what you've done because I do. Appreciate it. Thank you." I put on my jacket as if it were a slow motion replay, telling myself that if I walk out as advised, you will hold it against me in the balance. "I'm going," I say to the closed door of the bedroom and wait in vain the length of three heartbeats for a response before returning to the uncomfortable overstuffed chair to consider my next move.

We all seem to have eaten too much, sit in your living room in various stages of open-mouthed stupor, cups and saucers jangling on our knees, all except Elizabeth who is not in the picture. Every five minutes or so Hans announces that it is time to go, but he seems embedded in the couch. F has her eyes shut, waking herself periodically with noisy belches, distantly troubled by the rage of her digestive system. I have just talked myself into standing up when Elizabeth, appearing as it seems from nowhere, comes toward me. "I need a favor from you," she says. "Would you mind dropping me off at a hotel? I know you have a car with you or at least that's what I've been told." Roger interrupts, stepping into our as yet one-sided conversation before I can respond. "Don't be silly, Liz," he says. "You have a room here for as long as you need it." "You've both been much too kind," she says. "Really. I'd appreciate it if you backed off just a bit." "I'll give you a lift to wherever you want to go," I say. "Don't interfere in what doesn't concern you," Roger says. I don't recall throwing a punch at that moment but more than one person that witnesses the event corroborates that perception so I will only say in my defense that it was an unexamined impulse run amok.

The same police car that waved us on trails us, dogging our tracks, for a couple of blocks, though it's possible, I admit grudgingly, that its persistent presence is circumstantial. Another couple, slightly younger, hurries past us. "They're arresting people," the woman says. "Get off the street if you can." We run in their wake for a half a block, holding hands as we go. "This is the worst possible tactic," you say to me. "Slow down. Pretend you're talking to me. The last thing you want to show these people is that you're afraid of them."

"I don't have money to burn," Elizabeth says to me as I start the car and head downtown. "Do you know of a cheapish place that's not bug-ridden or anything?" I ask her how much she wants to spend, a question I never quite get an answer to. "No more than I have to," she says or words to that effect. The first two hotels I stop at are "too pricey," the third is "a bit skanky." The fourth has another not so easily definable problem. After the inspection of each unacceptable hotel, she apologizes for taking up so much of my time, the apologies accumulating. My tiredness, I assume, includes hers as well and in fact she yawns a few times between the fifth and sixth hotel possibility. It is only then, I want you to know, that I invite her to spend the night in the unused second bedroom in my apartment. "Oh," she says as if someone had put his hand on her ass in a public place. I realize after a moment or so of silence and the brief unexpected touch of her lips on my cheek that she has accepted my offer.

The phone is ringing inside as I struggle to unlock the door to my apartment. That it is inappropriately late for a call makes the receiving of it all the more urgent. "I'm frightened," the unrecognizable female voice on the other end whispers huskily after a moment of understated breathing. A wrong number, no doubt, and I am about to say so when the caller addresses me by name. "I know you understand what I'm going through," you say. "Would you mind returning? I need someone around I can trust."

At the corner, a police van appears and cuts off the couple that had run past us. We watch as they are handcuffed and loaded into the back of the van, which seems from my vantage to have a crowd of other arrestees already inside. We step inside an antique clothing store and you ask the proprietor if she knows what's going on outside. "I try to mind my own business," she says. "Do you mind if we hang out in here for a while?" I ask. The proprietor, who is a youngish woman with white hair, considers my question. "If you want to stay," she says, not looking at us, speaking very slowly, "you'll have to purchase something." While you go through the shelves and racks and barrels—I have offered to buy as a gift whatever you pick out—I check out the street activity. It is hard to see anything without making whoever cares to look from the streetside aware of me. I'm not positive of this but someone—a man in uniform perhaps—seems to be coming in our direction.

I have this idea as I unlatch the door to my undersized apartment that my guest room will seem as inadequate to Elizabeth as the various hotels she's rejected. I offer her a drink of something, which she politely refuses, as a delaying technique. "It's charming," she says, traversing the hallway to my small living room, taking possession of my favorite chair. "I may not be putting this right, but it seems to me wonderfully impersonal."

When I return to your apartment you are waiting at the door for my arrival or so I think because the door opens virtually the moment I punch the buzzer. We sit together on your couch for a while, your head on my shoulder. "My friend, I feel so much better now that you're here," you say. Momentarily, you fall asleep and we sit this way awhile, you sleeping awkwardly on my shoulder, your head increasing in weight by the minute. Finally, careful not to wake you, I lift you up and carry you like a child into the bedroom. It is only after I put you under the covers in the dark, wondering if it would be all right to lie beside you, that I notice a shadowy form in the arm chair on the right side of the room.

Elizabeth does not leave the next day or even the day after, is still in fact spending her nights in my guest room two weeks after her arrival the night of your dinner party. She has been looking for an apartment, she says, and has not been able to find something up to her standards at a price she thinks she can afford. You and Roger have gotten it into your heads, seem to take it for granted, that we're having some kind of torrid affair, which I've given up denying. I'm not sure myself what's going on between us, but it's not much. Roger calls here two or three times a week to speak to his sister and it is through his perception that I get your reaction to Elizabeth staying with me. You are furious with me, Roger says, and it is creating stresses in their relationship. "Elizabeth's no trouble," I say to him. "I should think not," he says, meaning of course whatever it is he means.

The cop looks in the window, but doesn't come in the store and why should he? We hang out in the shop another fifteen minutes, each buying something of negligible use—I get a pair of hand-knitted gloves, gray with an orange leather patch at the palm—before returning to the street. By this time, we've learned that there's been an unauthorized anti-war protest march in the vicinity, which explains the police activity and the random arrests. My idea is to move off in a direction that will separate us from the protesters, while you think we ought to show solidarity, even get ourselves arrested if that's the way it plays out, since we're in the neighborhood of the march anyway. And so we stand in front of the store, debating the relative merits of our positions in hushed voices. We end up, veering off in opposite directions, but after a couple of blocks, I decide—not wanting to seem a coward in your eyes—to turn around and go after you.

And then of course, for no reason I can understand, the thing I have been denying (or at least feeling privately innocent about), becomes, if I am to continue to see myself as an honorable person, undeniable. I say "for no reason I can understand" because I have not been attracted to Elizabeth, at least not insofar as I understand my feelings. And still it happens, the thing we'd been denying, and happens again. Elizabeth had knocked on my study door while I was working, something I'd asked her not to do, and then entered soundlessly before I had a chance to say "I'm busy" or "Come in," whichever came first to mind. "I want to say something to you," she said in a barely audible voice, which seemed to merge with the text I was working on. "Yes?" without turning around. "I'll come back when you're less busy. You've been so kind to me the last thing I want to be is a nuisance. You've probably been saying to yourself when is this person going to leave." By this point her aggressive self-effacement is beginning to wear on me. "Well …" I say. "It's true, isn't it?" she says. "You've hated having me here and you've been too discreet or whatever to let me know. At the very least, you ought to let me make it up to you. It will make me feel better." I thought she was going to suggest, as she had several times before, treating me to dinner or something of the kind and so I say, making light of her earnestness, "Anything that makes you feel better will make me feel better." And what could I have possibly meant by that. Inevitably, she misconstrues my remark—we misread each other and ourselves—isn't that the nature of misunderstanding—every step of the way. And that's the way the neurasthenic Elizabeth and I end up in bed together, each doing the other a presumed kindness neither wants nor appreciates.

I hurry after you while trying if possible to avoid police attention and think I see you a block or so away at the back edge of a group, marching under the banner DANCERS AGAINST WAR. It's not at all clear to me why some people are being arrested and others ignored. Even as I hurry toward you a van passes and I can see that the back is dense with protesters pressed against one another like a rush-hour subway car. And then, to my surprise, I see you running toward me and I increase my pace and we meet midstreet and embrace as if months had passed and not minutes since our last meeting. "We can leave," she says, "if you want. It was important to me that you came to get me." We walk off with our arms around each other, each carrying the plastic bag with our antique clothing store purchase in our other hand.

"It's nothing," you say in answer to the question I haven't yet asked. I stare at the shadow, perched in your armchair, trying in the dark to decipher who or what it is. Its continued silence seems to me ominous. "Would you turn on the light?" I ask, wondering at the same time whether that's the choice I really want to make. You hesitate. "It's very bright," you say. "You'll have to shut your eyes before I turn it on." I am reluctant to shut my eyes, so I offer to look away instead, which makes you laugh. "Just shut your eyes," you say. "It's no big deal. As soon as the light is on you can open them again."

Once the affair starts it has its own disconcerting momentum. It isn't that we're in love or even particularly affectionate with one another. It's just that the sex—the fucking—takes on an urgency neither of us seems able to resist, which makes getting anything else done virtually impossible. Since I work at home and Elizabeth has no job, the opportunity for sex is virtually endless. After the first encounter, Elizabeth moves into my room with my unacknowledged, perhaps grudging consent. The odd thing is, in that period between encounters—those increasingly rare moments when we aren't going at it—I long to have my apartment to myself again. But those feelings pass when she comes into my study and holds out her hand and says, somewhat shyly, "Do you mind …?" And then of course when I acknowledge to Roger that something is going on between us, he seems skeptical of my confession, says "Well, you said there wasn't anything going on and I took you at your word and where did that get me? Why should I believe you now?"

A cab drifts by and I hail it and we both get in. When the driver says where to, we both almost simultaneously, announce the address of the other's place. And then we look at each other and giggle foolishly. In any event, the driver takes off without further instructions and I wonder—I suppose we both do—which of the two addresses he has been given he has decided on. You whisper something to me that I can't quite decipher and we kiss, and we kiss, the kind of public behavior I find hateful in others. I let the moment take me where it will until self-consciousness sets in, and I become frightened, anxious perhaps, not at where things might go but where perhaps they might not.

Elizabeth is out, looking for a place to live—she is actually considering putting a deposit on an apartment she saw yesterday—when you call. The talk recedes from small to smaller to smallest and then, without preliminary, you ask if I could meet you for a late lunch today. "How late?" I ask, though it is not a matter of when for me but whether. "Twoish," you say. When I hesitate you say, "It may be difficult for me to get away from work. Maybe we ought to make this date for tomorrow or for some time next week." "Is there something particular you want to discuss?" I ask. "Not really," you say. "I do want you to know how happy it makes me to hear that you've been happy. You have been happy, haven't you? That's the word on the street."

The cab lets us off in front of your building and I trail you to the door. You don't ask whether I'd like to come in but the offer seems implicit so I follow you to the elevator and, after a mostly silent trip where we stand apart not quite looking at one another as if recreating our earliest beginnings, into your apartment which seems on its best behavior as if company were expected. "What can I get you?" you ask. "What are you offering?" I say. And that's when you come over and wrap your arms around me, punctuated by a sigh of exhaustion, and I wonder, not willing to ask, if that's your best offer.

I am assessing my feelings about Elizabeth's relocation—how much do I really mind? I miss her but I'm also glad to have my place to myself—when the doorbell rings unexpectedly. My imagination of possibilities doesn't extend any further than Elizabeth's return, for which I already have a predetermined response. So when you of all people appear looking like something out of one of my erotic fantasies in a long-skirted, apple-green summer dress, I am not so much disappointed as unmoored. "I called first," you say. "I tried to reach you but your line was either busy or something wrong with your phone." What else can I do but invite you in. "I can't stay," you announce as you step beyond the threshold, which I immediately translate into, *Don't expect me to jump into your bed.* "Where's Lizzy?" you ask. My answer is to glance behind me and offer empty hands. "I can see that she's not behind you," you say, which creates a momentary breach in the good feeling between us. "She's taken her own apartment," I say, which you no doubt know or you wouldn't have shown up as you have. "What a coincidence," you say. "Roger is moving out of my place as we speak."

It is as though someone or something rushes by me as the light goes on. When I adjust my eyes to the glare—for an extended moment I see only dots—we are alone in the room, an unaccountable salty smell in the air. You invite me to sit on the edge of the bed, mentioning only once and in an offhand way that intercourse after a D&C is out of the question for at least three weeks. "What can I do to make things up to you?" you ask, offering from under the covers a pale hand like a found object. "I'll take a rain check," I say, lying down next to you. "Forget it," you say. "This offer is only good until daylight."

It's the interludes—the moments of frustrating delay—that tend to ruin things. I am sitting on the edge of your bed in my boxers, catching flashes of my protruding gut in the wall mirror, waiting for you to emerge from the bathroom. I make a point of not looking at my watch, but I sense at least ten minutes have passed since you announced your imminent return. My hard-on nods and stretches in your attenuated absence, establishes a mourner's posture. Your large, feral cat, Isabella, pokes her way in and sniffs the air, checking me out from a protective distance. I hold out a hand in her direction, whisper her name. As an afterthought, having ignored me throughout, she jumps on the bed. That's the moment you choose to re-enter the room, wearing a lime-green silk bathrobe that I may have given to you on some forgotten occasion, much of your left breast making an uncredited cameo. "What's going on?" you say as Isabella bumps up against my shoulder. "I can't leave the room for a moment, can I?"

My interest in you, which embarrasses me all things considered, has in recent years been swathed in denial. "I'll lie alongside you," I say as if I were the one doing you the favor, which may also be true. My offer, though implicitly accepted, is not received with notable enthusiasm. You are tired of course, and wounded, have lost to perceived necessity, to sacrificial slaughter, your unborn living other self. There is no comfort I can offer to answer that loss particularly when only a few hours ago you welcomed it. And while lying next to you in your rueful, wounded state—what could be more obscene?— my penis stands warily on guard. Your hand notices. "My poor baby," you say.

"I'll have a glass and then I'll go," you say, your back against the closed door, still in your coat. "It'll be awkward, don't you think, if Elizabeth walks in on us." I edge toward you in a kind of willed slow motion, daring you to move out of my way. We crash softly against the door. "She no longer has a key," I whisper before almost kissing your ear as you avert your head.

I am wary of seeming too eager so I instruct myself in the art of indifference, wait with checkered patience for you to make the first move. It's not happening. We lie on our sides, facing each other from a modest distance. Finally, you seem to slip almost imperceptibly in my direction as if my greater weight had tilted the bed and, encouraged, I enjoin the space between us. A chaste kiss followed by a second peck, followed by its open-mouthed, tongue-stabbing sister and then I undo your robe in a kind of anti-intuitive dream act, parting the front before opening the belt. A nervous laugh escapes from your side of the bed, a childish giggle, a mousy squeak. A cry.

"I don't know if I want to do this at this time," you say, pulling me toward you with one arm, while holding me away with the other hand. "If you don't know, who does?" I say.

"Does that make you happy?" you ask from some beneficent distance.

It follows, doesn't it, it tends to follow, that when you get what you want, what you think you've always wanted—I'm speaking of myself here in the generic "you"—it isn't anything like you thought it would be. Why isn't it?

"I'd be happier if you didn't ask that question," I mumble in the denouement itself or just before I explode in your hand.

"Can you promise me that Elizabeth won't return?" you say. "I'm willing to promise anything if it will get me what I want," I say.

Then again there is the counter-productive pressure to perform brilliantly when I am with you so I am tempted to accept the ambiguous opportunity you offer me to gracefully withdraw. To back out while making it seem as if you are the one making the decision. Then it hits me, which changes everything, that you are the one making the decision.

"I want to be out front with you," you say. "I loved being with you, but I don't think we ought to do this again."

"As long as I have your word for it," you say. Every creak in the floorboards turns your head as if the only scenario that occupies you in the act of love is Elizabeth's return to claim her place.

"Doesn't it matter that I love you?"

Even as I take whatever risk you allow me, I feel myself backing off. "Do you love me?" you murmur or perhaps it is something else.

As we tangle, as I slide into you, *This is what I want* playing in my skull like a rediscovered tune, there is a knock at the door that repeats itself.

"Yes," I say under my breath, "yes."

I don't know what to say.

PART
II

SEVEN

———

It's a presumption, she thought, for someone you're no longer with and no longer love to write a book addressed to you. It's equally presumptuous perhaps to assume that an unnamed character with whom you share, if only metaphorically, certain behaviors is intended as you.

Still, who else can You be if not her? More than 50 percent of the character's attributes are hers or close enough. JB gets off on getting intimates seriously pissed off at him and she's hardly the rule-affirming exception. That's all she will say at the moment without her analyst in the room or at least an impartial third party, which excludes most of the people who've passed through the revolving doors of their story.

First things first: her name is V. Lois Lane. The V stands for Virginia and is only used on her driver's license. She is a former Lifestyle Editor of *The Daily Metropolis* and is currently Articles Editor for the hippest monthly on the newstands, *The Magazine*.

There will be none of the evasions of anonymity in her text, though she is a shy person, who tries to disguise her shyness by saying whatever comes into her head no matter how outrageous or indiscreet. She doesn't censor her conversation, that's not her style, because if she did, she sorely doubts she'd ever get anything said.

What the text provisionally called YOU never mentions is that Jay and I actually lived together for an extended disputed, depending on your source, period of time. The meeting in an elevator repeatedly, circumstantially, as a means of bringing us together is pure fantasy— or literary conceit if you will. Jay and I met through an ad in, of all places, *The New York Review of Books*. After I broke up with Roger, my childhood sweetheart and first husband—yes, his name was actually Roger—my sister, presumably concerned about my state of mind, took out a Personals ad on my behalf in *The New York Review*. The idea was to interview the various respondents until she found someone she deemed suitable for me and then bring us together in a way that would seem uncontrived. Delores was in a relationship herself at the time so there was bound to be some awkwardness inherent in the procedure.

Jay, who claims never to have answered a Personals ad before, was the fourth or fifth respondent and the first to pass Lorrie's test. Why it required six separate dates for Lorrie to settle on him as "perfect" for me remains one of those mysteries better left unexplored.

In any event, for their seventh date, Lorrie invited Jay to dinner to meet me, not mentioning to either of us at the outset the disguised intention of the invitation. In fact, we were both somewhat annoyed at the other's unexpected presence until Lorrie, during the dessert course, offered us a slightly fictionalized version of what she had been about. "This is my sister," she said as if that were title enough for anyone. "This is Jay sometimes called JB."

I have a confession to make before I go any further. I was the one, the well-meaning officious one who took the ad out for my sister, who had been going through a man-hating phase. Therefore the reason for the six dates was not quite the mystery I made it out to be earlier, though I was never really sure of my motives. Why hadn't I turned Jay over to Lorrie earlier? I can only give you my reasons at the time, which were these. There was something about him that I found elusive, even remote. Who was JB really beyond the pose of his self-presentation? With each date, I said to myself the next date will decide my course of action one way or another. And maybe—I'm not quite ready to admit this—I didn't want to relinquish him.

Still, when I gave the dinner in which the two of them met for the first time, I was clear about what I was doing, or clear enough. I stood up during the dessert course, which was an apple crisp (from a new, untried recipe) I had made for the occasion, and announced myself. "I have an explanation to make to you, Jay," I said. "The person I described in the ad you answered was not really me; it was my sister Lorrie. I'm sorry about the deception, but I knew Lorrie would never take an ad out on her own. So. Also, the bio I gave you about myself was Lorrie's bio and not my information—Lorrie is the actress who day-jobs as a dental hygienist."

At this point Lorrie interrupted. "This is unbelievable," she said in a mild voice. "What right did you have to do that?" Jay, I noticed, seemed unruffled, continued to negotiate his crisp, though at a more meditative pace. His indifference, if that's what it was, was more troubling to me than the anger I anticipated.

"I had hoped you would understand," I said to him. "The person you were interested in you only thought was me when essentially it was my sister, Lorrie. I have a good feeling about you two, I do. Anyway, I'm already in a long-standing relationship and I'd be bending the truth if I said I didn't love my partner."

By that time we were both staring at Jay waiting for him to show his colors.

He had to swallow and then wipe the corner of his mouth with his napkin before he could speak. We waited and waited to no avail.

"I have had it up to here with both of you," Lorrie said. "I'm going home now if there's no objection. If I stay, I'm likely to say something you'll both find unforgivable."

"I'll see you home," he said, getting up from the table, making a point of not looking in my direction.

"I think that's a good idea," I said.

"I'm not going anywhere with him," Lorrie said. "I got here by myself and I can see myself home or any place else for that matter."

After Lorrie left, promising to call when she felt better about things, Jay and I got naked together for the first time. It started with a friendly kiss. Afterward, he said, "Was that you as yourself in bed with me or you as your sister?"

I wondered myself, but I saw no point in acknowledging the question as worthy of response.

"Will I see you again?" I said to him as he was getting ready to leave. It was the kind of question that just asks for grief, but I uttered it despite myself, oblivious to better judgment, and so was stuck with the consequences.

"Whenever you want," he said, which might have been the most generous thing he ever said to me.

Nevertheless (it seemed only fair, didn't it?), I was prepared to hand him over to Delores if that's what they both wanted.

By the time Lorrie called, two days had intervened and I was in another place in regard to Jay, an emotional backwater hitherto uncharted. It was the tone of Lorrie's call that made me aware that I was now unwilling to accept the terms of the arrangement I had authored. When she announced with muted enthusiasm that all things considered she might be willing to get together with Jay for a drink some time, I said, "No, no, forget it, please. I made a mistake and I apologize for it."

*   *   *

Three months after JB and Lorrie started dating, Roger and I agreed to a trial separation., which from my perspective was merely a halfway house for ending our seven-year marriage. It was a few days after we double-dated with Jay and Lorrie that I found myself displeased with almost everything Roger did. I thought it can't be all my fault, can it, though it probably was and it had something to do with Jay. Whatever that something was I had been aware of it for a while without acknowledging it to myself. That was about the time that Lorrie was on the blower with me virtually every day, thanking me to obnoxious excess for bringing the two of them together.

On the other hand, Jay never called to thank me for delivering Lorrie to him. Was there a message there? Maybe he still hated me for having lured him into a relationship with someone else.

* * *

I was riding in the elevator up to work and I noticed the notorious novelist whose latest self-importance I had just completed and admired (while disliking) and I felt I owed him something, a smallish smile at least, for having bad-mouthed his book to an office associate. Anyway, we exchanged smiles as we were getting off at the same floor and I said to myself let's see where this will lead. I was up for a flirtation with this notorious chauvinist, something to make me like myself more, whatever it took to improve the weather of my self-esteem.

* * *

Lorrie announced over lunch at Zero's that she couldn't decide whether to move in with JB or not and then if she did (decide), whose place should it be, his bigger, hers better located and better put together. I entered the discussion with willed good faith as if we were not talking about a man I wanted (perhaps) for myself. "You know," she said, "when we were younger, I would hardly have trusted you concerning Jay." Funny that she thought that. My recollection was that she was the one—in high school in particular—who made a practice of going after boys who had shown interest in me first.

He asked me to stop by his place after work for a drink and I took down the information on the back of the *Publisher's Weekly* I was carrying, knowing (and not allowing myself to know) what it would likely come to. He had a carelessly nurtured reputation to uphold. The rest of the day I regretted having accepted his invitation, though I confess I was curious to see how he lived. The chance to eavesdrop on the secret life of his apartment was irresistible.

* * *

"Was this his idea or yours?" I asked Lorrie, who mused over my question before changing the subject. Her evasiveness indicated to me that the suggestion to live together had not come from Jay. Later she said, "He's been hinting in that direction but hasn't exactly gotten around to asking." "You barely know each other," I said, "but of course that doesn't mean anything." "You see that, don't you," she said, "that it doesn't mean a thing. I've always trusted your perceptions, Lois."

During the prolonged displaced courtship I had with Jay, I asked him a lot of questions about himself, which he seemed more than willing to answer. He seemed less curious about who I might be, but that may only have been because it was not the real me I had on the table. Of course he didn't know that then.

During lunch break, unable to cope with the wilted salad in front of me, I called Jay to ask his advice about Bill Worth's invitation. "I'm in the middle of a sentence," he said, "can I call you back?" "It'll have to be in the evening," I said, "when I get back from visiting Bill Worth's place. I don't take personal calls at work."

"I don't like the idea of you going to Bill Worth's place," he said. He had called me back at the office despite what I said to him about personal calls. "I can't talk now," I said, "but I appreciate your brotherly advice."

Bill's place was even more ostentatiously tasteful than I allowed myself to anticipate. It was also impeccably neat and, outside of the one room with book-lined walls, without much personal stamp. Even the paintings on the wall, mostly abstractions, some by painters whose names I didn't have to go to art school to recognize, seemed relatively anonymous. In all, it was a set designer's vision of a successful writer's apartment. He offered me a glass of wine from what he said was a very good bottle and, after giving me ample time to drain my glass, asked if I'd like to go to bed with him. I said, "No," and that was it. The subject was never mentioned again, though it was not an especially long visit. Forty minutes later when he saw me to the door, the feeling in the room was that he had been the one to turn me down.

That night, latish, after my uneventful visit to Bill Worth's Village apartment, Jay called, wanting to know if my virtue was still intact. He asked in fact if I was all right, but what else might that mean? "Why this concern?" I asked.

"I feel protective toward you," he said.

How would I have felt if Bill Worth hadn't asked? I wondered. Would I have lied to Jay had I accepted Bill Worth's offer? Questions concerning roads not taken tend to occupy me long after those roads are no longer on my map.

Jay was ten minutes late for our luncheon date at the Terror, a recently opened Middle Eastern restaurant with a provocative menu three blocks from work. Fortunately, I had a manuscript with me to edit, and I was marking it up with outraged queries to pass the time. When a man arrived, conspicuously out of breath from apparent running, I barely noticed his sliding into the seat opposite me, or at least I gave a good imitation of not noticing. We each waited for the other to introduce the not easily definable subject that occasioned this meeting.

"I've missed our lunches together," he eventually said, an intrusion on our discussion of some movie we had separately seen.

"I don't know if I missed you or not," I said.

"If you don't know then you probably haven't," he said as if it didn't matter to him one way or the other.

I couldn't help contrasting Jay's reaction to Bill Worth's. Bill Worth didn't really care a lot whether I accepted his proposition or not. You couldn't reject him in that situation because there wasn't enough of him at risk. On the other hand, Jay's apparent cool was obviously worked-up. Though I might respect a man who showed his vulnerability, I was never particularly attracted to whatever it was disguised as indifference.

I had the sense, like a buzz at the back of the neck, that I would say something to Jay—that it would flame from my mouth without premeditation—something so unforgivable that he would get up and leave the table and never talk to me again.

"What if," I said, "what if I told you I had slept with Bill Worth? Would we be here now drinking watery coffee?"

"Did you?" He took his glasses off to unleash his X-ray vision.

"Have you been sleeping with my sister?"

"What does your sister tell you?"

"We don't discuss you in that way. I suppose I don't want to know the answer or I know it already and don't want to think about it."

"So you slept with Bill Worth to get back at me for being with your sister, which, let me remind you, was your project in the first place."

"But I said I didn't sleep with Bill Worth."

He held out his hand and I grabbed on to it before it got away, a gesture in complete opposition to what I was feeling about him at the moment.

"Where does this leave us?" he said.

"Well," I said, "I'm not going to go to bed with you if that's what you think." In taking back my hand, I jarred my coffee cup with my elbow, about half of the cup overflowing its bounds sopping paper napkins in its wake.

"Why don't you just throw the coffee in my face?" he said, getting up, dropping some money on the table and walking out in a way that begged for a recall.

"Bill Worth's is bigger than yours," I called after him, turning at least one waitress's head.

That night, unable to sleep, I called my sister's number and hung up when Jay answered. My memory is short. But I couldn't remember having behaved so badly before. There were two consolations. One, that Jay was to blame, and two, that I secretly knew that I was a better person than the one on display.

A week later, Lorrie called and caught me in a less dangerous mood. It took twenty minutes of idle chatter before she found her way to the point of her call. "Don't take this the wrong way," she said. "Jay and I have decided it wasn't meant to be."

I felt immediately sympathetic and inexplicably anxious. "I'm so sorry," I said.

"I appreciate your saying that," she said. "I felt bad because you gave him to me as a kind of gift and I think it's just terrible to throw a gift back in the giver's face, but I think he preferred your imitation of me to the real thing. We were never really on the same wavelength."

"I don't think I ever understood what that expression means," I said.

When Lorrie took pains to explain the expression to me, I knew she wasn't suffering Jay's loss to any terrible extent. "Would you mind a lot if I dated Jay?" I asked.

"I don't know," she said, "I might. Could you at least wait a couple of months?"

I thought I could, but when it came down to it I couldn't. My plan was to let a month pass and then take it from there, call him or e-mail him, depending on how I felt at the time. It seemed to me a reasonable plan and I probably would have held to it if I hadn't impatiently phoned him three days after Lorrie reported their split.

It was not a random headstrong act, my call. I woke up during the night, taken in hand by a dream in which Jay came to the door to sell me the O-Z volume of an anatomical encyclopedia, which I refused to buy unless the A-N was also included. I asked myself: Why would Jay have broken up with Lorrie so soon after our edgy lunch unless he was sending me a message? The message, as I read it, was, "I'm available to you." It seemed only good manners to respond.

I had to call three times before I circumvented his answering machine and even when I got him live so to speak, my first impulse was to return the phone gently to its cradle. In answer to his bored "Hello," I said in a somewhat accusing voice, "Why have you broken with my sister?" And then, listening to myself in echo, I laughed crazily.

"Are you asking for yourself," he said, "or as a spokesperson for the local chapter of the dating police?"

"I won't do anything that will hurt my sister," I said. "If we're going to see each other—is that what you want? I hope so because it's what I want—we're going to have to be circumspect for a while. I hate lying, I do, but I don't want to hurt Lorrie. Do you want to come by tonight? There's a Moroccan takeout down the street that three different people have recommended to me."

He didn't answer right away, which I never quite forgave him for. "Am I really smaller than Bill Worth?" he said.

"Oh come on," I said. "I never saw Bill Worth's. I was just ..."

* * *

For three weeks or so, we got away with it or at least no one—certainly not Lorrie—let me know she knew what was going on. Many of our mutual acquaintances assumed she and Jay were still an item and it wasn't my business, was it, to tell anyone it wasn't so. My semi-regular conversations with Lorrie probably showed some strain, though Lorrie for her own reasons refused to notice. It was our habit to touch base virtually every other day and eventually

Jay's name popped up, Lorrie going back and forth in her feelings about him, mostly glad it was over, wishing he would call some time, aggrieved that he hadn't cared enough to try to patch things up. When she talked against him, even mildly, which was Lorrie's style, it was all I could do not to argue in his defense.

Deceiving your own sister is no fun or too much guilty pleasure for any decent person to acknowledge her exhilaration.

I didn't believe I was doing anything wrong, but I longed to confess, wrote Lorrie an apologetic letter which I very nearly posted.

In the end it was Roger who blew the whistle, mentioning it to Lorrie as a by the way, assuming (so he said) that she already knew.

"I don't think I'll ever talk to you again," Lorrie said to me on the blower and then stayed on another fifteen minutes to chat.

Right after Lorrie found out about us and stopped talking to me (except those times when she absolutely couldn't avoid it), Jay and I had a series of fights leading to a period of estrangement—a kind of irrevocable breakup—that lasted eight days by my count and nine by his.

We broke up again a few months later—this time for two weeks, a period in which we both dated other people—and after that we talked about moving in together.

There was a lot of possibly unfounded distrust going on between us, often taking the form of jealousy, and for our first six months together we kept looking for evidence (and finding it) of betrayal and bad faith. One thing I had come to know about myself was that if I didn't even the score with someone who had done me wrong (the melodramatic phrase says it all) I would be unforgivingly unhappy with us both.

It was an intuitive thing. I lived my life as if reprisal, or the threat thereof, was a necessary deterrent to betrayal.

An example: When Jay told me some old flame of his has invited him to lunch to ask his advice about some live-in boyfriend who no longer lived-in. I said it would make me unhappy if he went to this lunch.

"I'm not going to break this appointment because you're unreasonably jealous," he said. "I promise you it's just advice she wants from me."

"You don't have to go," I said. "You can't be the only source of wisdom in her life."

"I can't not go just because you don't want me to," he said.

I didn't understand why not and remain to this day thoroughly puzzled by his explanation.

So when he went to lunch with Francesca—I believe that was her name—I called Bill Worth at his unlisted number and teased another invitation from him to his apartment. After soliciting the invitation, I couldn't in clear conscience turn him down a second time, could I?

Some time later, wanting to heal the rift I confessed the Bill Worth episode. "I did it because you went to lunch with thing," I said.

We were walking in the street at the time, going to a dinner party at our friends, the Powers, and Jay turned his back on me and crossed the street. I crossed over, and when I caught up, put my arm around his shoulder, regretting everything particularly my confession. "I'm really sorry," I said, "but you know it didn't matter."

"I didn't sleep with Francesca," he said.

"But you might have," I said. "She probably wanted you to. You probably wanted to yourself."

He pulled away and stomped on ahead and I trailed behind as if we were attached by invisible wires.

We rode different elevators up to the party, or Jay walked up—I forget (I forget a lot of things)—the point being that we didn't talk all night. Or the next day either.

While I was at work, I called him at the place we shared, not to check up on him—that was not my intent the first time around---and got no answer. I called at a time he was almost always at his desk, writing—it was his habit, his willed commitment, to sit in front of his word processor for four hours every morning—so his not being there had its ominous aspect. I waited an hour, though it was a closing day on *The Magazine* and I didn't have time for craziness, and then tried to reach him a second time, and a third, and a fourth. So he was out and about, getting back at me. It wasn't so much that I was furious at him, which I suppose I was, as I was mortally disappointed. I mean, this is a man who has his hero say in a novel, "Everything is forgivable." On the other hand, I tended to believe that what isn't tolerable isn't forgivable.

I didn't ask him where he had been. I saw no point in inviting further deception. Instead, I only pretended to leave for work in the morning and instead hung out at the subway station—anyway, I had some manuscripts to read—and sure enough at a few minutes after eleven o'clock he appeared. Jay rarely noticed his surroundings and this morning he was even more preoccupied than usual so I had no problem following him without his being aware of my shadowing presence.

I was planning just to note the station he exited and then go on to work, but I had come this far so I got off the train—I had been in the car behind his—to see where the trail led. I had barely taken a step when he turned suddenly in my direction and came toward me, unaware of me until we were barely a foot apart. He seemed pleased to see me and we hugged before negotiating the issue of what each of us was doing there. My story was that I was meeting a writer but that I had confused the time. He offered no explanation, suggested we go somewhere for coffee.

We walked with our arms around each other and I forgot, let myself forget, the reason for my being here. After coffee, we hugged as though we were separating after an illicit meeting, a desperate extended hug, and, in love, I went off to work at *The Magazine* and he went ... wherever he went.

And when we came back together at home at the end of the day, I asked him in an unguarded moment, a teasing smile on my face, if he had been meeting another woman when we ran into each other.

He said, "Of course not," and I wanted to believe him, I would have believed him, I almost believed him.

"Then what were you doing on Chambers Street?" I asked.

"Does it matter?" he asked.

"It matters if you refuse to tell me," I said. All this was going on in a bantering, friendly way, though making me extremely anxious at the same time.

"Maybe you'll just have to trust me," he said.

"Or not," I said. "What would you have said if I had said the same thing to you?"

The conversation ended, as so many of them did the first year we lived together, when one or the other of us walked into the next room. It eased the tensions and made it possible for us to go on together.

I told Leo of the difficulties Jay and I were experiencing and he asked—Leo had also been Jay's therapist for a while—if I thought a joint session might be useful. I said it wasn't something I was interested in pursuing right now.

"Why is that?" he wanted to know.

I had my reasons but I was not ready to share them with Leo, whose natural sympathies were with the male figure in the relationship.

I bring this up now because Leo figures more importantly later in the story.

So we had no family counseling from Leo and we failed to talk through our problems, but after the first year, after my sister forgave me and Roger came back into the fold as a friend, we settled into a routine of comforting conflict. Leo would say in later years that we swept our problems under the rug, but for a while there it seemed as if the metaphorical rug had kind of lifted off the ground on its own.

Anyway, that's my version of the story of how we got together.

EIGHT

This was the first (and she hoped, last) ad she took out in the Personals section of a magazine and she wanted to put her best foot forward without setting up her respondents for disappointment. This was the second draft: "40ish woman, sometimes thought beautiful, creative, cunning, quirky, with advanced degree in English literature, wants to meet intelligent man between 30 and 50,who listens more than he talks." In the third draft, she dropped "sometimes," replaced "cunning" and "quirky" with "original" and added "feeling" between "intelligent" and "man." She also added, "Right wing zealots need not apply," but then decided "intelligent" and "feeling"—maybe change feeling to humane—would obviate against closed-mindedness. Still, she barely recognized herself in the description she was issuing, which concerned her only for the limited time she thought about it.

Before placing the ad, she called a few friends on the phone and read them the possibly final draft, writing down the best of the suggestions for improvement, though turning in the notice pretty much as was. As soon as the Personal was out of her hands, as soon as it appeared in the paper, the whole business filled her with revulsion. She vowed to herself not to pursue the matter.

But when a few days passed and an envelope arrived with twenty-seven responses and two days after that, another with nineteen more, making it—addition had never been her strong suit—forty-five or forty-six in all, she piled them on her desk and began to read them like an eavesdropper or, more to the point, like an editor.

Some she discarded after reading a line or two. An ax murderer with a good prose style was preferable in her view to an uninteresting mind. More often she read them from beginning to end and found herself mildly curious as to who the writer might really be behind the calculated disguise of his prose. She warmed to those writers who avoided salesmanship and were just a little self-deprecating. At some point she found herself sorting them into piles.

The discards were filed away under the categories, Bores and Serial Killers, sometimes mutually inclusive. The third category, the survivors, found themselves under the all-purpose rubric: Others. She let a week pass before reassessing the nine surviving respondents.

The first one she read, the one arbitrarily sitting at the top of her "Others" pile, moved her but she couldn't say why afterward. When you looked at it with a cold eye, it seemed barely a cut above ordinary. She put it aside, then read two others that were much cleverer, and a fourth that had a distinctive if unlikable voice, then returned to the first.

It was not so much the letter itself that needed revisiting as her uncharacteristically sentimental response to it. Its appeal was in the kind of risk the author seemed to take, though the letter was pseudonymous, signed, of all things, "Lonely on Livingston Street." The second (or was it third?) reading moved her almost as much as, perhaps even more than, the first, and she wrote an e-mail letter in response. She might have phoned—he had also given her his phone number—but it seemed appropriate to take small steps, small sure steps, rather than throw herself headlong into something she might later regret.

Dear Lonely on Livingston Street (she wrote),

I admired the directness and simplicity of your letter, and I was touched despite my native skepticism by your undisguised defenselessness. I will try to offer the same spirit of openness in return. Very few of the men I've known would have had the courage to make the kind of admissions you have openly offered in your letter. I know from personal experience how desolating loneliness can be, but it's also important—I hope you see this as I do—to be independent and self-sufficient. Being with someone in a mutually-fulfilling relationship is desirable, but a relationship should not be used like wallpaper—you see that, don't you?— over disintegrating walls. I've been there too. I'm beginning, I know, to sound a bit psycho-babblish here and I apologize or, to be wholly honest with you, don't apologize. I am a bookish person who prefers movies to theater, chamber music to opera, conceptual art to traditional painting—I know what I like and my tastes tend to be passionate. Still, I try to be open whenever possible to what I don't know. I have the capacity to change my mind, though sometimes it takes awhile. People tell me I am an intuitive person and it pleases me to think so. My politics tend to be liberal, but I also tend to vote the person—that's the intuitive part—over the apparent issues. I come from Baptists on my mother's side and atheists on my father's and my own religious leanings lie somewhere in between if such an unlikely territory exists.

If I sound like the kind of person you'd like to meet, I'd appreciate receiving another letter from you.

Yours sincerely,
Caring and Companionable in Chelsea

And those were the first volleys of what turned out to be an extended correspondence between C&C and the man who signed himself Lonely on Livingston, whose name, he eventually confided, was Saul. Two and a half months passed before they made an appointment to meet the following Friday night—it was her idea not his—and she wondered as the time got closer if she had set herself up for disappointment.

They agreed to meet at a café on the outskirts of Soho at 6 o'clock, each to be dressed all in black to facilitate identification. The first plan was to wear yellow carnations in their buttonholes, but the idea was more clichéd than she could bear and since she had just gotten herself a new black sweater, the in-black plan was a last-minute modification. No matter, it was still too "Shop Around the Corner" and therefore a tad embarrassing.

In any event, she wanted to observe Saul first, see what kind of appearance he made no matter the beauty of his spirit, before she presented herself. To this purpose, she arrived ten minutes late and peered warily through the blue-tinted window of the café. A little more than half the tables were occupied, mostly in groups of twos. There were a few single women waiting apparently for dates or husbands, but not an unattended man (dressed in whatever color) waiting for a woman in black. Saul had seemed so eager when she suggested the meeting and yet, unless there had been some mix-up regarding the place, he had seemingly not turned up. More likely, he was just delayed. A meeting postponed as long as theirs was fraught with all kinds of anxiety. Instead of entering the café and taking a table, she decided to walk around—look into shop windows—to give Saul opportunity to arrive at Café Retro before she made her entrance.

She was four blocks away when she hurried back, not wanting to make Saul feel that he had been deserted. Again, she peered through the window to assess the crowd. This time there was a man seated by himself, a man of Saul's age perhaps, which he said was forty-seven, interestingly ugly if something of a pudge, but he was wearing faded jeans and a dark blue (almost black) turtleneck. He was studying the menu as if he were trying to decipher a coded message.

She entered the restaurant and walked slowly past the man's table, before seating herself at the vacant one adjacent to his. He had not looked up when she passed him, which meant what? She was in no mood to guess. Which meant most likely that he was not expecting someone. Or, as his correspondence indicated, he was painfully shy.

It was only after the waitress arrived to take his order that he raised his head. She looked over and smiled and the man (Saul?) nodded to her in acknowledgment.

Collecting herself as it were, menu in tow, she edged over to his table, but his head was down again and she had to clear her throat to attract his attention. "May I join you?" she asked, a question he studied a moment without answering. She tried again. "Are you waiting for someone?" she asked.

"I've been waiting for someone all my life," he said.

That confused her, but as she was already in the process of joining him, she took a seat. "You're not dressed in black," she said.

He gave his clothes a surreptitious glance before answering. "I guess not," he said.

The waiter was hovering so she ordered a decaf latte and a blueberry-apricot tart while her companion glowered at the menu in apparent disappointment. He eventually settled unhappily on a medium-rare burger and an iced tea. "These places never have what I want," he said.

"What do you want that they don't have?" she asked.

"That's just it," he said. "I never know what I want until I see it on the menu."

"And so there may be nothing that you want," she said. "Or something so out of the ordinary ..." She left the sentence unfinished rather than say something impolite.

After about a half-hour of missed cues and mostly non-sequential conversation, she began to look over her shoulder for the possible emergence of the real Saul. And yet every once in a while, her companion would allude to something that very possibly referred to some matter from their five-month correspondence. It was disconcerting, and she considered asking him directly who he was, but the context, if there was one, restrained her. She liked the way their mutual shyness played off against the other.

"I don't usually invite myself to other people's tables," she said or told friends she said after the event, or non-event, was over.

"I never thought you did," he said, finishing his hamburger before she finished her tart.

When he got up to leave, he offered his hand to shake, wiping it thoroughly with his napkin before presenting it. The gesture seemed to parody itself, but she played along. At least that's the way it happened in the story she told to her handful of confidantes.

Saul was silent—no e-mail from him the next day or the day after that, no apology, no explanation—and she assumed (what else?) that this episode in her life was concluded.

She spent a few restless nights concocting scenarios as to why Saul had stood her up, the worst of them infiltrating her dreams, and then she willed herself not to think about him at all.

The following week, out of some impulse she didn't understand, though perhaps it's the nature of impulses not to be understood, she revisited the café she had been to the week before. She had hoped to show up at the same time as last week, but the impulse to revisit, which took over at the last possible minute, delayed her arrival.

There were no hesitations, no peering through windows, this time around. She merely entered the café as if she was meeting someone there (well, she was, wasn't she?) and headed directly toward his table.

She was all but positive that the man sitting alone at the same table with his back to the door was the same man she had joined last week and she took the seat across from him before discovering to her unacknowledged embarrassment that it was someone else altogether.

"How are you doing?" he said as if he knew her.

"Do I know you?" she asked. "You do look familiar."

"I was wondering the same thing myself," he said. "Jay." He offered his hand, but she had already gotten up.

"I thought you were someone else," she said. "Sorry."

"I am someone else," he said, "but you're welcome to stay. There aren't any other free tables."

She hesitated, was about to turn around and check out the room, but that seemed rude and so she slid back into her seat.

It was the same ritual as last week except with a different partner and at the end of the meal, Jay, if that was his real name, insisted on taking her check.

"I'm the intruder," she said. "I ought to buy you lunch." She held out her hand, expecting to be rebuffed but instead found herself holding both checks.

"I'll leave the tip," he said.

They walked out of the restaurant together and she said goodbye at the door, thanking him in her coolest manner for the pleasure of his company. Nevertheless, he walked along with her to the next corner, oblivious to her well-mannered dismissal of him.

"When will I see you again?" he asked at the corner.

She smiled, less at him than at the opportunity he was offering her. "Never, I hope," she said, and instead of walking off as she planned, putting as much distance between them as possible, she waited for a response.

He seemed momentarily dismayed, though that may have been an illusion encouraged by expectation. In the next moment, the post-dismayed moment, he put his hand on her shoulder and urged her gently toward him. It all happened so fast or so slowly she didn't have time to react or then again had too much time. Then he kissed her on the top of the head as if she were his niece for godssake, and moved off.

"Hey," she called after him.

After a moment's hesitation, he dutifully turned around and seemed to be returning without actually moving toward her. Then she realized that it was she who was approaching him. "Why did you do that?" she asked, arms crossed in front of her. She took no enduring responsibility for the belligerence in her tone.

He shrugged, then apologized half-heartedly and walked off. If she hadn't felt compelled to get back to the office, she might have gone after him and given him the shaking he deserved. She hadn't met a man she disliked so much in the longest time.

Lois developed a theory that Saul 1 and Saul 2 were somehow in cahoots with the probably pseudonymous Jay, who appeared at the same table Saul 2 sat at the week before. No acceptable explanation offered itself. Of course gratuitous nastiness could explain almost anything.

She promised herself that she would not return to the café at the same time the following Thursday, but when the time came she could barely keep herself from turning up. She had lunch in at her desk and read ten pages of a new Nadine Gordimer novel, actually reading five pages twice so as not to lose her way.

When she announced to her therapist that she was proud of her restraint he seemed unimpressed. "If it were me, I would have been curious to find out who was going to show up this time," he said.

"I don't like being the butt of someone's deranged idea of a joke," she said.

"How can you be sure it's a joke?" he asked.

"I just know," she said, regretting what seemed now like a missed opportunity.

The next day she appeared at Café Retro at the usual time—this time she was actually five minutes early—and found her table occupied by three women. There was no one there she recognized; eventually, she took a table by herself in the back.

It was one of those days when nothing on the menu appealed to her so she settled for a Caesar Salad and a Bloody Mary for her lunch, the salad to make herself feel virtuous and the drink as a reward for suffering the constraints of virtue.

If she were a food critic, and she had done some restaurant reviewing in the past, the salad would have gotten a C-plus/B-minus, losing points for the packaged croutons. For a second or two, she harbored the illusion that someone was casting a pall over her salad and eventually she looked up to see a familiar figure hovering alongside her table.

When he took a seat before asking permission and without invitation she realized that what she thought was a second anchovy had only been an aspect of his shadow. "Do you mind?" he said.

And what if she did? "Yes," she whispered. Though she had not forgotten her instinctive dislike of him, she was also, if unexpectedly, glad to see him.

"I'd all but given up running into you again," he said.

"This is not my usual place," she said. And then she told him as economically as possible, the story of the two Sauls, searching his face to see if any of this was news to him.

The story seemed to confuse him and he questioned her on several of the details, seeming to miss the point or make something else, something more elaborate and complicated, out of it altogether.

"I'll tell you why I don't believe your story," he said. "Someone like you would never take out a Personals ad."

His presumptions knew no bounds, she decided, though perhaps his remark was meant as some kind of oblique compliment. "Why wouldn't somebody like me take out a Personals ad?" she let herself ask.

If she were pressing for a compliment, if that's what it was— she had the idea that she was trying to decode him—she should have known in advance, shouldn't she, that he was hardly the kind of person to honor such unworthy requests. "You just wouldn't," he said.

She laughed at the persistence of his evasiveness. On the other hand, she tended to believe that he was on to her in some not easily defined way. Though she had of course taken out the ad, it was an uncharacteristic gesture. "Thank you, I think," she said.

"If what I said translated into a compliment," he said, "it was not exactly intended."

"What an obnoxious thing to say," she said. She found herself eating her barely tolerable salad in slow motion so as not to finish before his order even arrived.

When the waiter asked if he might remove her plate, which had three orphaned leaves and a crouton remaining, she waved him off. There was work still to do. Ignoring the tempting fry dangled in her direction, she choked down the last leaf of grass, and mopped up the dregs of the dressing with a wedge of bread. Noting that he was halfway through his chicken and mozzarella sandwich, she signaled the waiter over, ordered a cup of coffee and studied the dessert menu as if she might be quizzed on it afterward.

"What looks good?" he asked.

"I never order dessert," she said. "Reading the description is pleasure enough."

After he claimed the check, getting no resistance from her this time around, she got herself together to leave. She expected him to ask for her number while planning to deny his request, the language of her refusal gradually forming itself in her mind.

"See you around," he said.

Their encounter felt incomplete and she continued to sit across from him, imagining herself telling him that he was so not her type, he was beyond hope of alteration. It annoyed her no end that he refused to give her the opportunity she had been anticipating. "Well, goodbye," she said. "I forget your name."

"Sometimes I forget it myself," he said.

This time, leaving the restaurant more or less together, they went off in opposite directions. She couldn't help feeling somewhat insulted by his decision to honor her feelings in regard to him.

At therapy that evening, she talked about the incident with Leo, who seemed inappropriately amused at her account. "Let me get this straight," he said. "You're angry at this man you barely know because he didn't give you the opportunity to hurt his feelings."

"When you put it that way," she said, "it makes me sound like a bad person. All I wanted … well, maybe I did want to hurt him a little. He was so arrogant and he led me on. Anyway, I don't have to ever see the son of a bitch again."

"And unless you return to that café, you probably won't," Leo said. "So what is all this anger about?"

She was disappointed at Leo for being less than his most perspicacious self. "If you think it's because I'm interested in that, you're barking up the wrong tree this time around."

He was silent for a change, gave her one of his severe looks. "Did I say that I thought you were interested in this guy you went back to the restaurant a second time to see?" he said. "I don't recall saying anything of the kind. If this guy doesn't matter, let's talk about what does. In any event, I'm the person you're angry at now."

"I don't like it when you manipulate what I say," she said, struck by the recognition that she had said the same thing almost verbatim two sessions ago. "I'm not angry at you, damn it." Hearing herself, she smiled ruefully. The guy does matter in some way, she thought, unwilling to say it, unwilling to let the thought linger. But he shouldn't. "Can we change the subject?" she said. "OK?"

The following Wednesday, she went back to Café Retro with a colleague who had never been there before and was disappointed not to see her tormentor at his usual table.

About halfway through the meal—the food less inspired than the PR she had given it—she noticed the man she thought of as Saul 2, eating alone about five tables away. She got up abruptly, excused herself (or didn't) and sidled between tables with exceeding grace (she imagined) to ask the question that had been obsessing her.

She had to clear her throat to catch his attention. "Oh hi," he said, looking up, held by the short leash (she thought) of some hugely diverting internal life.

"Do you know a man about your age with a reddish beard who calls himself Jay?" she asked.

"No," he said too quickly. "I don't think so. Should I?"

She didn't know him well enough to accuse him of being a liar. "I don't know if you ever told me your name," she said.

"I guess I didn't," he said.

"Look, if you see Jay, would you give him a message for me?" she said. "Would you tell him …?" But there was no message she wanted to leave and besides the reluctant messenger seemed to have retreated into the sanctuary of his inner life. She returned to her table without saying goodbye.

Was it the next day? More than likely several days passed before she got the unexpected phone call she had somehow been waiting for. The voice was familiar, though not so familiar that she placed it immediately. "I understand that you wanted to hear from me," he said after first establishing that she was no other than herself.

"Now that I hear your voice," she said, "I'm not sure that I do."

"OK," he said. "Look, I've been invited to a book party tonight—I'm not good at phone invitations—but if you're into crowds and finger foods, I wouldn't mind having you along."

"I don't know," she said. "Who's the writer?"

"It doesn't matter," he said. "You never heard of him. If you don't want to go, we can do this another time. Or never."

"You bring an exceptional lack of grace to even the smallest things," she said. "Will you pick me up or do I have to meet you there?"

"I don't mind picking you up if that's what you want," he said, "though I think it might be more fun if we arrive at the party separately and pretend to be former lovers who had just run into each other after twenty years apart."

"Uh-huh," she said, almost amused by the idea. "And for whom are we performing this childish charade?"

A compromise was negotiated. He would pick her up at *The Magazine* and take her to the party—that is, take her to the building in which the party was taking place—and one of them would go on up while the other would walk around the block or go across the street for coffee before making an entrance.

The problem was, their agreement hadn't stipulated which of them would do which and they got into a mild dispute on arrival when Jay suggested that she go up first. "I think I'd rather be the one getting the cup of coffee," she said.

She could tell that he was not very adaptable because he worried the issue for almost a minute before offering a grudging, "Fine."

So it was settled, but then she thought maybe it was better after all for her to be the one to go in first. "If someone asks," she said, "who do I say invited me to the party?"

"No one will ask," he said. "Probably a third of the people there will be crashers."

"Who invited you?" she asked.

"I wasn't exactly invited," he said. "My agent suggested I come. You want her name? Her name is Marianna Dodson and she's also what's his name's agent, the guy for whom the party is being made."

"I know Marianna Dodson," she said. "We've never met but I've talked to her on the phone and we've had e-mail exchanges."

"So this is what we'll do," he said. "You'll present yourself to Marianna and when I notice you talking to her I'll come over and she'll introduce you to me. And you'll say we've met, but that it was a long time ago and I'll say I remember but you'll be skeptical. We can improvise from there. Did I tell you how much I like what you're wearing?"

She waved him off and went into the building, noticing someone she knew slightly in the group going in ahead of her, a writer who had done a piece for her a while back.

Once she got into the crowded apartment and talked to a few people, some of whom she had met before, and got herself a glass of white wine, she let Jay's scenario for her slide out of mind, though she looked around for him every once in a while, made uneasy by his absence.

Finally, an hour or so into the party, she spotted him for the first time, standing at the edge of a conversation between two men, neither of whom she knew, and she smiled in his direction but went unnoticed or ignored. She edged her way over, crossing his line of vision, and stood by his side, waiting to be noticed. He continued to ignore here.

"I believe we've met," she said when he turned toward her, smiling without recognition, taken aback by her presence.

"Of course," he said. "Anyone who'd ever met you before would not forget you."

"I can see you don't remember me," she said, looking around her to see if anyone was listening in. "It was a long time ago. It was in another lifetime really." Four or five people seemed to be eavesdropping on their conversation.

"Of course I remember you," he insisted, but she could tell that he was bluffing and she was not inclined to let him get away with it.

"OK," she said, "What's my name?"

A woman came over—his agent she assumed—and took Jay by the arm, saying in this annoying way that there was someone she wanted him to meet.

She took his other arm, and said in the mildest of voices, "He's meeting me at the moment."

"And you are …?" the agent asked.

"Lois Lane," she said.

"Of course," the agent said. "Marianna Dodson. We've talked on the phone a number of times. I'm so pleased to meet you in person. You know, I thought I recognized the voice, but I wasn't sure. I didn't want to say anything until I was sure."

"This man and I knew each other twenty-one years ago and haven't seen each other since," she said. "I can spare him another twenty minutes."

Marianna Dodson apologized for intruding and seemed to back away, absorbed by the crowd.

Twenty minutes later when they caught up with each other again their meeting had the aura of fateful good fortune.

What else could they do but leave the party together, their story, or snatches of it, bruited about in the shadowy corners of the room where only the eavesdropping imagination could overhear.

Once they had established a past, there was no point in denying themselves a present. She spent the night in Jay's apartment and when she left in the early afternoon of the next day it had already been arranged that they would meet for dinner that evening.

Four months later, she sublet her apartment and moved into his place, which was marginally larger, for the short term. After a while, when his place began to seem oppressively small, they sublet a house together in Prospect Heights, a yet-undiscovered Brooklyn neighborhood in the throes of gentrification.

Two years later, when they found themselves caught up in an escalating, unacknowledged battle of wills, the word marriage insinuated its way into their dialogue.

NINE

In the revisionist version, after sharing an apartment for three years, they agreed in principle to get married, a fight-reconciling decision on a motoring trip through Canada that came hard on the heels of an agreement never to see the other again after they got back to the States.

The decision, a triumph of last ditch desperation, represented a rare unanimity but it was not without attendant issues. As Lois saw it, they needed to decide as quickly as possible whether to have a real wedding (and consequently who to invite and how many) or whether to get married on the road by a justice of the peace. Jay said it was all the same to him while she said that she would abide by his choice.

"I can go either way," he said.

"I don't care for big weddings," she said, "but don't you think the nature of the ceremony might have something to do ultimately with the quality of the marriage itself? As a case in point, Roger and I knew our marriage was doomed when the minister that married us—and he seemed a serious man at the time— ran off with the daughter of one of his parishioners."

"I think I like the idea of getting married on the road," he said.

"Do you really? Why?"

"Well," he said, "if the minister misbehaves after the fact, we'll probably never be the wiser."

What he said made no sense to her though in the spirit of accommodation, she let it pass without comment. "If you want to get married on the road, if that's what you really want, sweetheart," she said, "then that's what we'll do. Is that what you really want?"

"I want to do whatever pleases you," he said. "Would you look at the map to see where we might cross over into the U.S."

She groaned. "You know how I hate reading maps. Isn't it enough that I agreed to marry you? If I have to look at the map to make that happen, I'd just as well keep things as they are."

They had had this conversation before or some variant of it and he wondered if whatever fight was in the offing, and he was dying to tangle, might be prevented if he kept his cool in the face of irresistible provocation. For no good reason, he turned left at the next intersection and after several miles of uninhabited desolation turned left again. That they were lost, or so it seemed, and that it was her fault, irritated him to distraction. And then, out of seeming nowhere, a sign appeared: US Border—14 mi.

"You see," she said, "you can get anywhere you want without my having to look at the map." Her flickering fondness for him returned in momentary abundance.

During the customs interview, when asked if they had anything to declare, she told the guards that they had crossed the border the other way just a few hours ago and were returning to the States to get married before resuming their trip. Before she could complete her story, the pleasanter of the two officials asked them to pull over to the building on the right. For the next several hours, their car was taken apart and their belongings ransacked.

They sat on a couch in the hut on the side of the road, holding hands during their detainment, glancing through the window behind them from time to time to see what progress was being made. There was an extended period during which nothing happened while the official assigned to taking apart their car took a lunch break.

Jay paced the room, suddenly impatient, feeling claustrophobic.

She got up after a while and walked alongside him. "Are you thinking the same thing I am?" she asked.

He finessed his answer. "It's not worth it," he said.

"Coward," she whispered back.

When they were told they could go, she said to the woman official, who had initially seemed sympathetic, "Don't you people have anything better to do with your time?"

Later, when they were on the road again, she thanked him for protecting her from her worst instincts and he had to turn away from the road, in momentary risk, to see that she meant it.

In some way it changed nothing. In almost every other way, it put a favorable light on all the things that disturbed her about being together. They got married at a justice of the peace in Presque Isle, Maine, the ceremony only unforgettable in its total absence of memorable detail. And then they recrossed the Canadian border to continue on the trip they had planned and unplanned during their carefree, bickering single days.

They both agreed that the ceremony was mercifully unpretentious and that, no doubt, they could have done worse.

They spent a day and an overnight in Montreal and Quebec City en route to Nova Scotia, doing the recommended sights along the way with a kind of bemused, disinterested patience, idiot grins on their faces (grist for unseen photographers) as if they were on a real honeymoon and indeed genuinely absurdly happy.

*   *   *

Two months after their return, the honeymoon glow barely faded, she discovered herself obsessively attached to someone else. This invasive presence in her life was a handyman hanger-on at the gym she went to dutifully on Wednesday nights, and was not like anyone else she had ever liked before. And if that weren't enough reason to avoid him, the man was either obnoxious to her or showed no apparent interest, which she took as interchangeable provocations. He had a reputation, which she didn't wholly credit, for groping women indiscriminately. The nasty stories circulating about him in the gym engendered— she despised the women telling the stories— a kind of perverse sympathy.

One night, later than usual, doing her repetitions on the stairmaster, angry at Jay for reasons yet to define themselves, she noticed that the only other person in the gym was the same narcissistic, muscle-bound creep, his name Luther, she had been fantasizing about. Though behind a desk on the far side of the room, a book open in front of him—she imagined the pages blank or a pornographic comic book secreted inside—she had the sense that he was inhaling her every move.

Where had everybody else gone? The important thing was not to show him she was afraid. Fear, she had read somewhere or heard said or instinctively knew, was catnip to the pitiless. She noticed on the wall clock—she must have dozed at some point—that it was 10 minutes short of midnight and the clock seemed hardly to be moving. She toweled off in a kind of slow-motion, though she had long since stopped sweating, put her coat around her shoulders and promised herself to walk past the dragon without so much as glancing at him.

She was already by him when he spoke. "Goodnight sweetcheeks," he said in a barely audible voice.

Outraged, she spun around to confront him. "Who do you think you're talking to?" she said. "I could report you for that. You know that."

She imagined him laughing at her but instead he said nothing, his thuggish face in the book he had armed himself with, the title registering subliminally as she left the gym as *Persuasion* by Jane Austen, one of her favorite novels.

Jay was asleep when she came in at whatever impossibly late hour and she had to wait until morning to answer his prying questions with the partially true, almost convincing story she had over-rehearsed the night before on the slow subway ride home.

"OK," he said when she had finished with the story and it felt to her like a slap.

"I don't like you questioning me like that," she said. "You make me feel like a criminal."

"No one can make you feel like a criminal," he said, not quite looking at her, "if you don't already feel like a criminal."

She walked away, then came back, came up to him from behind and tapped him on the shoulder. "If you are accusing me of something," she said, ruing each word, "I think you ought to say right out what it is."

"You've been accusing yourself," he said, stepping away, willing to let her escape.

"I told you what happened," she said. "I fell asleep. If you can't trust me, if you're going to be jealous over every little thing... Sometimes, Jay, you really piss me off, you know?"

"I'll take that under advisement," he said, a poor exit line he privately conceded, not at his best when under attack.

They made up in bed that night, or seemed to, each apologizing in turn with exaggerated conviction, their urgent lovemaking like the Hollywood movie of itself.

She went to sleep happy and woke with intimations of despair: her marriage to Jay had nowhere to go but down. And then Jay made it worse, confirmed her in her worst premonitions, by suggesting she give up going to the gym on Wednesday nights.

In fact, she had already decided not to go the following week, but Jay's bullying demand made it difficult, virtually impossible, to follow through on her decision. Whatever was going to happen, he had, if unwittingly—the evidence filed away for future debate—brought it on himself.

He was awake on her return from the gym the following Wednesday, lazing like a slug on the living room couch, watching a basketball game on television.

"I see that you get your exercise through empathy," she said, passing him by on the way to the bathroom. Out of the corner of her eye, she noticed him glancing at his watch. She had made up her mind, no matter what, that she would make no excuses for the lateness of the hour, would make no attempt to account for herself at all.

There was no making it up this time around. He lay with his back to her in bed, his anger like a force field between them, which might have frightened her if it wasn't so absurd.

She turned on the reading light next to her side of the bed, asking his permission without expecting a reply, and leafed through an old *New Yorker* lying on her end table. On page seeventy-seven, he got up noisily and disappeared for awhile. She dozed, though kept the light on at the same time, feeling betrayed by his prolonged absence. She thought of calling out to him that she had done nothing that needed apology, but it wasn't a stance she felt comfortable with at this hour of the night.

For his part, Jay spent the remainder of the night on the couch, wide awake, wondering if the problem, suitably ignored, would go away of its own accord.

The following Wednesday, without making much of it, she decided to forego her weekly gym appointment. She thought she'd surprise Jay, picking up a couple of overpriced steaks from Balducci's on her way home, and she felt thwarted not to find him where she left him.

She looked around for a note, some explanation as to where he had gone, not expecting to find anything—why hide a note if he wanted her to see it—but carrying out her intention with meticulous concern for detail nevertheless.

She fell asleep before he came home and woke during the night to find him in bed sleeping restively next to her. A mix of anxiety and outrage occupied her for the next couple of hours and she ended up cuddling against his unforgiving back.

In the morning, she made a point of not asking him where he had been—she would not be the one to pry—storing her grievance under a display of uncharacteristic early morning cheerfulness.

He seemed thrown off his game by hers and she could tell he was just dying to market the version he had worked up of where he had been and what he had done. And then she actually kissed him goodbye like some prototypical housewife (except it was she who was going off to work) before leaving him for the day. He clamped her to him and she felt the tweak of his neediness, which brought her more confusion than comfort.

"I love you," he said rather desperately as they came apart, which was not a usual part of his routine.

When she was away from him, safely out of the house, it amused her to imagine what he made of her performance, though she had only the thinnest notion herself of what (if anything) was going on between them. It was a game of denial, the game itself denied, in which the one who showed the least concern won the as yet undetermined prize.

She never told him she had come home early that Wednesday— while he never volunteered why he had been out late that night— and the following week as a matter of course she resumed her routine at the gym. Jay was always part of the landscape, sometimes waiting up for her, sometimes dozing on the couch, when she found her way home.

It was six months later, after Luther had broken with her, which brought her a mix of relief and self-doubt, that she turned her attention once again to Jay. One night after lovemaking, perhaps even during the act itself, she found herself longing to confess her brief insignificant affair with Luther, clean the slate as it were, but some wary inner voice wouldn't allow it.

In the third year of their marriage, it may even have been the fourth, over dinner at the most expensive restaurant they'd been to that wasn't on someone else's expense account, Jay confided awkwardly during the appetizer course that he had fallen in love with another.

The news itself was less surprising than the confession and she weighed its implications on the balance beam mediating despair and hope before offering a response.

"Is it anyone I know?" she asked.

"Well," he said and she out-waited the unnatural silence for him to continue.

"I feel terrible," he said, which evoked a laugh with claws.

"That's too bad," she said. "So who is this person?"

"I'm not planning to leave right away," he said. "You know that these things happen whether we mean them to or not. This doesn't have anything to do with you. My feelings toward you haven't changed."

"I think I'd be happier if you moved out as soon as possible," she said.

"I understand your position," he said, attending to the mostly uneaten food on his plate.

And then, with that out of the way, if not actually settled, she asked again who it was, her next breath contingent on his unwelcome news.

And still he refused to tell her, which was less forgivable, she decided, than the betrayal itself, whatever it might be.

Clearly, it was someone she knew and she made a list at work of possible suspects, the list in order of uncertain priority extending itself to fourteen.

A week passed with no change in the situation—Jay still living in what increasingly she thought of as her place, the issue that occupied their lives barely mentioned since his confession at the restaurant. In fact, they had hardly talked at all since then, each making a point of avoiding the other while having their dinners together at the same kitchen table.

That night when she came to bed, he was already there—his reading light conspicuously on—doing the crossword puzzle. "If I made a guess," she said, "would you at least tell me if I was right or not?"

He seemed to be considering her question, though what he said next gave no indication of it. "I want you to know that I've stopped seeing her," he said. "That's what I wanted to tell you. I can't promise that I'll stop thinking about her, but I won't see her again. I also want to say that I appreciate how patient you've been. You've been wonderful about everything."

Was that meant as an apology? she wondered. His presuming on her forgiveness made her want to smash him over the head with the first object that came to hand. "It's too late for apologies," she said in a quiet voice. "Your breaking it off or her breaking it off, whatever, doesn't change the fact that you're not welcome here."

He gave her a pained, little boy look. "I want to stay," he said.

It was hardly the appeal she had hoped for, not the one in the best case infinitely variable scenario she had been carrying around all week in her imagination. "I'll think about it," she said. "But I absolutely want you out of my bed."

If he was a gentleman, which he clearly wasn't, he would have taken his sorry ass into the guest room down the hall without a moment's hesitation. That he hesitated, that he seemed to be considering her non-negotiable demand was more than any reasonable wronged person could bear. "I'll tell you what," she said, "if you tell me who it is, I'll let you stay for the night—I know the guest room is an unholy mess—but tomorrow I want you out of here. All things considered, I think that's a generous offer."

"C'mon, you know who it is," he said without actually moving his lips.

"If it's who I think it is," she said, "I'll never forgive you. That's a promise."

He turned on his side away from her, said something she couldn't decode, which might have been "Of course not" though probably wasn't.

She aimed a kick at his back, though by the time it landed it barely moved him from his vagrant spot. A second kick was considered, held sway briefly in the platonic realm, but it never quite translated itself from conception to deed. The hand of sleep intervened.

When she woke up, the dusty light of the unborn morning flooded the curtains. It took a moment for her to notice, that moment following the moment she recalled the disturbing interchange that preceded sleep, that the huddled figure on the other side of the bed was missing. She wondered if he was really gone, anxiety rubbing elbows with her brief elation, her feelings on his absence not yet quite in place.

"I continue to love you," he said rather desperately as they came apart, though this time it was in the interstice between sleep and waking, a wistful echo from a momentarily forgotten dream.

TEN

Now that Jay had agreed to the joint session with her therapist, she couldn't remember why she had favored the idea in the first place. It was one of those things you did, which is what she told Lorrie over the phone, so that afterward you could say you had done everything (or something) to save your dying marriage. She wondered if she had ever loved Jay—that is, she could no longer remember having loved him—but there was something between them, some intricate bond, that seemed resistant to violations no matter how unforgivable.

All she wanted, after all, was to get free of him and then afterward they could salvage or not whatever dregs of their relationship remained.

Jay, on the other hand, said he was willing to change if necessary to save their marriage.

"No one changes after forty-five," she said.

"Who said?" he said.

"I can't remember anyone who has," she said, dipping her toe briefly into the well of memory. "Can you?"

"Maybe what we're talking about is not the incapacity to change," he said, "but a failure of memory."

She hated it, totally despised it, when he pretended to be smart.

At the same time or perhaps a moment afterward she had a quiver of recollection—a subliminal flash—of having felt something other than indifference for him.

For their first session, they sat in parallel chairs about twenty feet apart facing the therapist who was in an impressive high-backed armchair in a slightly elevated part of the room.

"Is there some agreement as to who goes first?" Leo asked, looking at neither of them in such a way as to give each the impression of being the one he was urging.

Jay was the first to speak. "I don't mind if she starts," he said.

"I'd prefer going second," she said. "He's the one who believes in talk."

"In that case," Leo said, "that's the way we'll do it. So Jay, what's your view of why your marriage isn't working?"

"Why does she get to go second?" Jay said. "Is it because she's a woman?"

"I thought you were both in agreement as to the order here" Leo said. "When you offered her the opportunity to go first, I assumed you took it to be the favored position. If it wasn't, why did you make it sound as if you were doing her a favor?"

"Because that's the way he is," she said.

Leo gestured for her to stop whatever else she was planning to add. "Let's hear what Jay has to say, shall we?"

Jay stood up, collected his coat but then seemed to change his mind from whatever to whatever. "You're both right," he said. "I'm a terrible person and I'm choked with regret."

"That's a bit easy," Leo said. "Don't you think?"

"I'm sorry about that too," he said. "I tend to let myself off too easily and I'm sorry. OK?"

"He isn't really sorry," Lois said.

"You're probably right about that," he said, "but look I'm really sorry that I'm not really sorry. What about you, LL? Is there anything you're sorry about?"

"That's not a real question," she said, "and you know it. Do you want me to say that I'm sorry I married you? All right, I'll say that I'm sorry I married you."

Leo looked around as if there were another person in the room with them, possibly dangerous, he hadn't seen before. "Let's stop here," Leo said, "and we'll continue next Wednesday at the same time."

Jay, who had been standing, his coat folded over his arm, sat down. "We haven't even decided who goes first," he said.

While Jay wrote the therapist a check for the truncated session, Lois mumbled "Thank you, Leo," and made her way out the door.

There was an antique shop a few doors down and she occupied herself studying the unusual face of an oversized wall clock in the window, figuring Jay would be out in a few minutes and they would travel back on the subway together. She didn't see him come out, though sensed his approaching presence, feeling a sugar rush of affection for him. arming herself with a slightly ironic remark.

For his part, Jay noticed his disaffected wife waiting for him and decided to cross the street to avoid her, pretending to the unseen observer that he was in a huge hurry to get somewhere.

When on turning her head, she noticed him rushing from her, she wanted to call out that she was not as frightful as he imagined.

* * *

SECOND SESSION

"If anything's going to get accomplished, we're going to need to give these meetings some structure," Leo said. "Lois, I'm going to ask you to speak for no more than five minutes. At which point, Jay can either respond to what you've said or use the allotted five minutes to present his own grievances. On the second go around, I'd like you each to address what the other has said. Are there any questions before we begin? ... If not, let's get to it. Lois."

"It's easier if I get up," she said, though she remained seated. "I don't think I'll need five minutes to say what I have to say. Actually, I don't know why I am here. For a while now, I kind of thought, that despite our persistent problems, that it was worth making whatever effort was necessary to continue, to get along. I no longer feel that way. That's all. Well, one other thing, whatever feelings I once had for Jay are gone. It's like one morning, they put on their coat and scarf and went out the door. I feel my own growth as a person has been inhibited by this marriage. That's all. I don't want it any more. I don't want to be in this marriage. That's all I have."

Leo seemed to be waiting for Jay to continue, but after a few minutes he pointed his finger at her, who seemed to be looking the other way. "Jay?"

Jay stood up. He had something written on a card that he held up in front of him. "I was going to say that I would do whatever I could to keep us together, but that seems foolish now, doesn't it?" He sat down, resisted putting his head in his hands.

Leo looked over at Lois, who made a point of avoiding eye contact, and waited for someone, perhaps even himself, to break the silence. "It might be useful," he said to her, "if you were more specific about what you want and feel you're not getting from your marriage."

"What I want, OK, is that Jay accept the fact that the marriage is over," she said.

"Why should Jay's acceptance or not make a difference?" Leo asked her.

"It just does," she said.

"She wants to hurt me," Jay said, "but in a way that protects her from feeling bad about herself. She hates the sight …"

Leo was quick to intervene. "Let her speak for herself please," he said. "The two of you seem to know more about the other's feelings than your own … I understand that your feelings about Jay are intuitive, Lois, but it would be useful here if you gave some examples of what seems to be the problem."

"He doesn't want to hear them," she said.

"Then tell them to me," Leo said. "I want to hear them."

She had a hundred grievances against Jay, she had a litany of grievances—they often came to mind unbidden like the hypnogenic lyric of some ancient detergent commercial—but at the moment she couldn't come up with one that didn't seem hopelessly trivial. "He's only interested in me as an extension of himself," she said.

"That's not specific enough," Leo said.

"He doesn't clean up after himself," she said. "He leaves crumbs all over the apartment, which I end up having to deal with."

"What do you say to that?" Leo asked, turning his attention to Jay.

"I'm not sure what you're referring to," Jay said.

The role she was performing laughed. "You see what I mean," she said.

Leo reiterated in paraphrase Lois's complaint about his messiness.

"She's probably right about that in general," Jay said, "but I've been better about it recently. I think even Lois would acknowledge that I've been trying."

"Too little, too late," she said.

"Let's put this into perspective," Leo said. "If, say, overnight, Jay no longer left messes that he didn't clear up, became a sudden exemplar of neatness and consideration, would that alter your feelings toward him?"

Lois wanted to say that it might, but since she didn't believe it, felt the dishonesty of any such assertion, she said nothing or rather mumbled something that was susceptible to a near infinite variety of interpretations.

"What Leo's saying," Jay said, "is that the example you gave represents a petty annoyance and is hardly a significant factor in your disaffection toward me."

"I don't think that's what he's saying," she said. "Is that what your're saying, Leo?"

"Is there anything Jay can do or not do that would make you reconsider your decision to separate?" Leo asked.

"What about her?" Jay interrupted, suddenly outraged. "Why is this whole discussion about my changing?"

"There's nothing he can do," she said, "nothing that would make the slightest bit of difference."

"I hear you," Leo said. "Jay, what changes would you like to see Lois make?"

Jay started then stopped himself. "Well, for openers," he said, "she can stop fucking Roger or whoever it is she's been seeing on the sly."

Leo seemed unfazed by the revelation. "And if she stopped," he said, "would that make a difference?"

"I'm sorry I said that," Jay said.

"What are you sorry about?" Leo asked. "It was something you felt, wasn't it? You meant it, didn't you?"

He looked over at Lois, who seemed to have shut down. "I didn't want to embarrass you," he said.

"I thought you thought I was shameless," she said and seemed, until she took a deep breath, on the verge of giving into feelings she was hours away from acknowledging.

*   *   *

THIRD SESSION

They arrived at the therapist's office together and Jay suggested that she go in by herself and that he would loiter in the lobby of the building, kill a few minutes, before making his appearance.

"You're joking, right?"

"Well, I don't see any reason to throw Leo off his game."

"As Leo would tell you, and as I'm sure you know, that's exactly what you do want. Denial is a form of admission. What's Leo's game in your opinion?"

"I'm here to find out," he said.

She laughed. "Shouldn't we tell him things are better?"

"What do you think?"

They entered Leo's office at the same time, though not quite together, made their appearance in single file, Lois the first to enter.

As they sat down in their respective seats, Leo looked over his glasses from one to the other, then jotted something down in the small notebook he always seemed to have on the table in front of him. "People, I'd like to try something a little different today," he said. "I'd like to have you switch roles—Lois you take on the role of Jay and Jay you present yourself as Lois—for the next twenty minutes."

Lois looked skeptical while Jay seemed vaguely amused.

"So Jay, putting yourself in Lois's shoes, I'd like you to present your grievances toward your husband ..."

"She wears a seven-B," Jay said. "There's no way I could get my feet in them without cutting off my toes."

Leo ignored him. "And Lois," he said, "I'd like you to begin to imagine yourself as Jay. I'll give you both a few minutes to focus and then Lois—that is, Jay as Lois—will start. Otherwise it will be the same format as last week. Once we start, I'd like you both to stay in character. Any questions?"

"I don't know, Leo," Lois said. "I'm not comfortable with this."

"Let's give it a try, OK, and see how it goes," Leo said.

"I'd prefer standing," Jay said slyly, getting up then sitting down. "One of the things about Jay that makes my hair curl is that he is incapable of empathy. That's all I have to say at the moment."

"Jay," Leo said, pointing to Lois.

"Lois tends to be a perfectionist," she said, "and so tends to be what I call hypercritical. The way I see it, there's nothing I can do to please her no matter how many times I apologize for being oblivious. She has an idea how people should be and if you don't live up to that idea, you're in trouble. You never know exactly where you stand with her."

"Could you give us an example of what you mean?"

"An example? Well, one night after a hard closing, she comes home from work and finds me sprawled out on the couch., watching TV, a basketball game most likely, and she says something like, 'You're supposed to be working on your book not watching TV, aren't you?' And then it comes out that I'd neglected to do the little bit of shopping she had asked me to do and I get some more grief from her. I don't answer and then I offer an unfelt apology, but when she keeps at it I put my coat on and go out for a walk. Some hours later when I come back I find her talking on the phone to someone I think I have reason to assume is her lover."

"How does that make you feel?" Leo asks.

"How does that make me feel? I let her know how angry I am by knocking over a few chairs and then I order her to get off the phone. It's not the best way to handle it but I have to do something and I haven't the faintest idea what else to do. I'm bigger than she is and I don't see why I shouldn't get my way."

Jay waited a few minutes before speaking. "Look, I'm not going to let myself be bullied by him in my own house. I have a right to talk to whoever I please. His behaving like a jerk only makes me more determined. His bad behavior, which I may have provoked—you get to know the right buttons—is embarrassing to me. He knows I hate scenes. And so I get off the phone, which makes me hate him even more but not before telling my friend that I'll call him back."

"Do you ever after the dust has cleared talk about what went on?" Leo asked Lois.

"Not usually. Mostly we avoid each other. One of us goes in the bedroom and the other stays in the living room."

"What happens the next morning?" Leo asked Jay.

"I don't as a rule talk much in the morning and when we do talk we tend to be excruciatingly polite as if one wrong word might cause irreparable damage."

"Do you have breakfast together?" Leo asked Lois.

"I ... excuse me ... Lois doesn't eat breakfast. She has coffee and sometimes a toasted bialy but it's not a sit down breakfast. On the other hand, I have designer cold cereal in the morning and tend to read the sports page while making music chewing my granola."

"If you don't discuss your fights, how do you ever reconcile your differences?" Leo asked Jay.

"Time heals," Jay said, "and sometimes it doesn't."

Lois cut in just as Jay was completing his sentence. "My policy is to ignore problems and hope they go away," she said.

"When I feel wronged, I can be absolutely unforgiving," Jay said, "and it's possible that Jay has been burned too much to be willing to risk making a gesture he knows will be scorned."

Lois pursed her lips. "I guess when the going's tough, I don't have much backbone, do I?"

Jay picked up a flyer that had been lying on the table and folded it into a paper airplane.

Leo's bearded face showed a minor crack of concern and he suggested after Jay had launched the paper airplane in Lois's direction and Lois had stared daggers at Jay in return that it might be a good idea to stop the role playing at this point and return to their former selves. "I'll give you a few minutes to get back into your own heads."

"This was useful," Lois said. "When he was going on about me being hypercritical and unforgiving, I got the impression he was really talking about himself. I learned something from that."

"Hey, weren't we both talking about ourselves?" Jay said.

"You're so clever," she said. "Why hadn't I ever noticed that before?"

"You're the princess of snide," he said. "Look, I'm sorry I threw the plane in your direction. It wasn't really meant to hit you, it was to make you aware there was someone else in the room."

"You never say anything that means anything," she said. "Why is that? You are the prince of self-justifying incoherence."

Jay got out of his chair with apparent difficulty as if fighting some kind of invisible resistance, and retrieved his coat.

"Why don't you just leave?" Lois said.

Leo turned his head just enough to glance at the clock on the wall. "We still have some time left, people," he said.

* * *

FOURTH SESSION

There is no record of a fourth session.

PART
III

ELEVEN

After our fourth and final breakup, six years and nine months pass uneventfully before I run into you again.

During this prolonged separation, I make little or no attempt to get back together with you or even to see you on other terms, or rather whatever limited attempt I make to see you is made without urgency or passion or rather my urgency is worked up, a way of convincing myself of feelings that may no longer exist. The motor of habit ran my train and when it broke down my pursuit of you accordingly stopped in its tracks.

If we are ever to get back together, I tell myself—you see I do occasionally reconsider the unthinkable—it will have to be as if we were both different people. It is not that I woke up one morning no longer in love with you as that I consciously, willfully, put my romantic longings aside and chose to live in the prosaic real world. In the past when we separated it had seemed to me part of some larger unintelligible process working toward some transcendent reconciliation.

My childlike father used to tell me—it was as if I was eavesdropping on a conversation he was having with himself—that maturity meant no more than the ability to accept things as they are.

So in order to pass as an adult in the world's collective imagination, I acknowledge that it is over between us. We are done, burned out, canceled, history, finis, a page irrevocably turned. That's my passing-for-an-adult mantra.

* * *

So, outside of dreams, which I can't control, you no longer exist for me. (That is, you didn't exist until I started to write this novel in which you persistently disappear only to reemerge.) There are two ways to look at it. I'm either trying to win you back or to exorcise the tidal pull of my feelings for you forever. I can't help but wonder—it is an essential part of the game—if you're reading these words. I imagine that you are, which is next door to, or at least down the street from, to the same thing.

Let's start this section again.

Four and a half years have passed since our fourth and theoretically final breakup and I am in San Francisco to give a reading—actually a series of readings—from my novel in progress. I go out to dinner with my host and his wife at an old-fashioned plush Victorian-style restaurant, an old standby which has recently come back into favor. During the dessert course, I take a break and visit the men's room in the hope of recovering sufficient appetite to contend with the *tarte tatin* awaiting me at my abandoned place.

That's the setting—plush restaurant in downtown San Francisco—for your next unanticipated appearance in my life. As I step out of the men's room, focused on my apple tart, a woman who bears you more than a circumstantial resemblance has just emerged from the facing bathroom. It is clearly you—I recognize you from the back of your head, I'd know you anywhere—though of course it can't really be you. You're on the East Coast, working as an editor for a trendy monthly journal called *The Magazine*.

I watch whoever it is return to her table and the profile she shows on sitting—the partial profile—is close enough to yours to produce a disturbing frisson. You are with another woman, someone I've never seen before, and I observe the two of you in conversation before returning to my untasted dessert and a brandy my hosts have ordered for me in my absence.

When we exit the restaurant a half hour later, you and your companion have already gone, but then I notice you on the street waiting by yourself for a cab. I make my excuses and separate from my hosts, not sure yet what I intend. Before I can reach you, you give up your vigil and walk off in an abstracted, daydreamy way. The choice makes itself. I decide to follow in your tracks at an unobserved distance.

My discreet pursuit goes on for longer than I had any reason to anticipate and in a direction virtually opposite that of my hotel.

It is as if you can sense my presence. At some point, you stop abruptly and turn toward me.

As I approach, you look around warily to see if anyone else is within call.

"Have you been following me?" you ask, reading my face without recognition in the shadowy light.

"I was planning to say hello," I say.

You take a wary step closer. "Hello? Why would you say hello to me? Do we know each other?"

For a moment, I'm willing to believe that I've made a mistake, but apart from the hair styling, it's hard to imagine that there is another person on the planet that looks so much like you. "You look almost exactly like someone I know," I say.

"Uh huh," you say and we walk along together in your direction. "This isn't some kind of pick up line you use, is it? Some alternate version of 'Haven't I seen you someplace before'?"

"How long have you been living in San Francisco?" I ask.

"Doesn't matter," you say. "I promise you I'm not who you think I am."

"But if you're not, how do you know who I think you are?"

When we get to Eureka Street, you stop. I hold out my hand, which you ignore. "I'll say goodbye here," you say.

"I'd like to see you again," I say. "Would that be possible?"

You offer a skeptical smile, which I don't pretend to understand. "I don't know," you say.

"Look," I say, "I'd like to take you to dinner. It would make me happy to take you to dinner."

The odd smile makes a second appearance. "I don't know you well enough," you say, "to be concerned about your happiness one way or another. I don't mean that to be as harsh as it may sound. This just doesn't make any sense to me."

I tell myself to walk away but obsession takes charge and I say, or rather hear myself say—my intention insofar as I allow myself one not to plead—"Please."

You turn your back on me. "Sorry," you say and wait for me to disappear before moving on to your residence, which is in a green frame house on the corner at the far end of the block. For now, it is enough for me to know where you are hiding out.

Early the next morning, I take a cab from my hotel room—I thought of renting a car but street parking is difficult in San Francisco—and get dropped off a block past your street. I don't want you to think I'm stalking you so I station myself as far from your building as possible while still having an unobstructed view of your front door. At 9:33 you come out of your building—a man and a woman had preceded you—and you start walking almost directly toward me. I have no choice but to duck into an alleyway to avoid being discovered. When I return to the street you are nowhere to be seen. I can see that I've managed this badly.

I go into the anteroom of your building and note that there are three apartments. I write down the names, Wooden, Margolis, Titianni—names that mean nothing to me—in a notebook and return to my hotel.

That evening, I give a reading in a hip independent bookstore and in the audience, an almost unacceptable coincidence, is the woman you were with the previous night in the restaurant.

To extend the coincidence, the woman you were with approaches after the reading with a copy of one of my books to be signed. It is almost—take this lightly if you will—as if fate is offering me another opportunity. "Who should I sign the book to?" I ask. "It doesn't matter," she says. "Just sign it." I look up at her as I return the signed book. "You know, I think I've seen you before," I say. "Is that right? Where would that have been?" "You were having dinner at Ernesto's sometime after nine last night in the company of another woman." "And you noticed us? I'm flattered or at least I suppose I should be." There is something edgy about her that doesn't ingratiate, but I nevertheless invite her for a drink in the high end café next door, an offer she neither accepts nor declines. When, eventually, the line of buyers uses itself up, she is standing by the door in her coat, waiting for me.

* * *

In the course of asking your apparent friend about herself, I manage to slip in a few questions concerning her companion, who I continue to assume is you. While A—the initial on the pocket of her blazer— nurses a peach margarita and matches my evasiveness with her own, I drink fizzy water with a slice of desiccated lime attached to the glass like a name tag. There exists what might be called a mutual dis-empathy between us.

"She's a recent friend," she says, "though not a close friend, a coworker with whom I share certain sympathies. We've only known each other a short time. Our eating together, well it has to do with a bet, the circumstances of which you don't want to hear about."

"What is it you both do?" I ask.

"Why is it I have the feeling you have an ulterior agenda?" she says. "Why don't you just tell me what you want to know and I'll decide whether I want to give you that information or not. OK?"

I make a quick decision, regretting my lack of discretion even as I confess to A that my interest in her friend, in you, comes from an uncanny resemblance she has to someone I've known.

"And you want to know whether my friend is who you think she is?"

"Will you help me?"

"For one, I don't know if I can. And for two, I don't know you well enough to know what you'll do with the information once you have it."

"I'm not sure myself what I want," I say. "I had no interest in seeing her again until, in fact, purely by chance, I saw her again. And now I don't want to let her out of my sight."

"What you're telling me is that you're behaving compulsively. That's not the best recommendation to earn my trust. I think I'd better go now."

"Look, you have my book. I've been completely honest about my understanding of what's going on. So you know something about me. On the other hand, you've given me nothing back. If you can assure me that your friend has been out here for more than six years and therefore cannot be the woman I think she is, I promise to walk away."

"I wish I could," she says. "Believe me, if I could give you that assurance, I would. The problem is, the very real problem is, that I suspect that my friend, as you call her, is probably the person you think she is. I am in no position to say more than that."

That's her exit line and I sit inertly by as she leaves the café. When she is gone, I notice that she has dropped or left behind a business card, which I retrieve from under her chair.

The card reads as follows:

ANGELINA WOODEN, PSYCHOTHERAPIST
Sanity is my business.

Group sessions. Alternate Therapies.
Private consultations. Insurance accepted.

401-246 1130

I am scheduled to return to New York City the next morning and I call the airline to change my reservation to the following Monday. Later in the day, I call Angelina Wooden at the number on her misplaced card, speak to someone else, a receptionist possibly— the voice oddly familiar—and make an appointment to come in for a consultation at three-fifteen the next day.

I'm acting on the possibly false assumption that the card was left for me intentionally.

If the two of you work together, there's the chance anyway that I'll run into you or at least learn more about what's going on at Angelina's place of business.

Though I'm open to being surprised, what happens next has little to do with the surprise I allow myself to anticipate.

The receptionist, a young man, keeps me waiting in the impersonal anteroom for no apparent reason—I am on time, I am the only one there—before sending me in to the therapist's office. The first surprise is that the woman behind the closed door is not the person I had coffee with after my bookstore signing.

The second surprise is that the therapist awaiting my entrance, making notations in a leather-bound appointment book on the desk in front of her—the two surprises are virtually simultaneous—is the woman that resembles you.

I wait in vain for you to recognize me before speaking. "How are you today?" you say, looking directly at me, giving nothing away.

"Are you sitting in for Dr. Wooden today?" I ask.

My question seems to amuse you. "Why would you think that? Who do you think I am?"

"I think you're whoever you say you are," I say.

"For both our sakes, I hope so too," you say. "And what's your story?"

Unsure of where to take this unacceptable exchange, I answer your question by reciting a version of the plotline of my novel.

"I am a man who is obsessed with a woman who has been in and out of his life in a variety of contexts, a woman he imagines he loves, a woman to whom he is addressing a letter in the form of a novel with some hidden purpose in mind that he has yet to understand and hopes to have revealed to him through the process of the telling."

"The thing is, with obsessive people," you say, "while they believe they're giving away their innermost secrets, they're really telling you next to nothing about themselves. I think we should pursue this. If you can come in tomorrow at one forty-five, I can give you a full session." You make a notation in your book as if I had already agreed to your terms.

I try unsuccessfully to see what you have written in the appointment book. "Will you be here tomorrow if I come back?" I ask.

You laugh at that in a way that seems rehearsed. "The only way to find out," you say, "is to show up."

*   *   *

There have been times—I admit this freely—when I've had difficulty distinguishing between dream reality and whatever else there is. I stay up much of the night trying to piece together into some kind of useable order the events I've just described. And the question that I keep coming back to, the inadvertently inescapable question, is what do *you* think is going on? Just who do you think I am?

The next day I arrive more than an hour early for my appointment and park at a diagonal across the street from your building, hunkered down in my car like a private detective, though with a notable difference. I am hoping to discover something that I don't know, that I'm not clever enough to know, that I'm looking for. No one enters or leaves the building during this first period of my vigil. The blare of a horn distracts me. A police car is parked alongside me without my being aware of its having arrived. The policewoman sitting next to the driver instructs me through gesture to roll down the window, which I do.

"Good morning, sir," she says, leaning out her own opened window and waits for me to acknowledge her before getting down to business. "Sir, what are you doing here?"

"Killing time," I say. "I'm early for an appointment."

"I have no problem with that," she says. "Sir, this is a 'No Standing' zone so I'm going to have to ask you to move along."

At that moment, I notice two women exit the building, one of whom might be you. The police car, which obstructs my view, makes the identification uncertain.

I offer what I hope is an ingratiating smile. "I'll be gone in a few minutes," I say.

"Sir, I'm afraid you'll have to move now," she says. "As my chief likes to say, 'The law waits on no man.' There's no reason not to tell you this. We've had a complaint about you. It's in your best interest to move along, especially if your reasons for being here are as innocent as you make out."

"Can you tell me the source of the complaint?" I say.

The head, that had briefly retracted, returns out the window. "Sir, don't you know when someone is doing you a favor? Get the fuck out of here."

As soon as I start up the motor, the police car backs up, giving me another open look at the building. A stream of people seem to be exiting, the lunch crowd perhaps.

When I drive off, I pick up the police car in the rearview mirror, moseying along behind me. It may or may not follow me in to the multi-level underground parking garage three blocks away.

I park the car on the cusp between level 8A and 8B—the first available space—and take a crowded elevator up to the street floor, my journey interrupted by multiple stops, the foul air circulated by a small ceiling fan that makes a whining noise with every revolution.

When I arrive at the building on Stetson Street, when I finally get an elevator to take me to the ninth floor and present myself at the Alternate Therapies Office of Angelina Wooden and Associates, I am ten minutes late for my one-forty-five appointment.

The same male receptionist admits me, though seems not to remember me from yesterday. I mention that I am here for an appointment with Dr. Wooden.

"She's not here," he says. "Dr. Wooden does not come in on Tuesday afternoons."

His news is disappointing, though not wholly unexpected. "She told me to come back today at 1:45," I say, giving him my name, which he insists is not in his book.

I take a seat, suddenly aware of being tired. "I'll wait," I say.

"Didn't I just tell you she won't be in this afternoon? If you leave your name and phone number, I'll see that it gets to her."

I can't explain why I ignore his request other than it seems important not to give in to him. I pick up a random magazine from the rack to my left and browse through the glossy pages.

I doze off, skip-reading an overheated article in a four-month-old *Sports Illustrated* about the otherwise unheralded importance of tight ends in the West Coast offense. When I open my eyes there are two cops standing over me, one of whom is the woman that rousted me from my vigil across the street. I look over at the receptionist, who refuses for obvious reasons to meet my glance.

My first impulse is to make a run for it. Instead, I get to my feet and move in virtual slow motion out the door to the elevator stand. The moment I ring for it, an elevator arrives, three people out of the five already ensconced making their unhurried departure. By the time I get inside the elevator, the two cops have also edged their way into the car.

The cop, who hadn't spoken to me before, who is possibly also a woman—it is not wholly clear—cautions me to stay close when the elevator releases us.

There are five people waiting for us to exit, one of whom, the one in the back behind the hugely tall man, is you.

"They told me you weren't coming in today," I say as you stride by without looking in my direction on your way into the elevator.

"Oh hello," you say, acknowledging me with a perplexed smile.

At the last possible instant, the door in the process of sliding shut, I force my way back into the elevator. (Always elevators in our story.) "Stop him," a voice calls out, a woman's voice, though it is possible that these are random sounds that I particularize gratuitously.

So think of us riding up together in this Art Deco elevator, standing side by side, several other passengers who may or may not be aware of our story standing about like extras in a movie to complete the picture.

By the time we reach the ninth floor, we are the only remaining passengers.

"The police are certain to be looking for you here," she says as the door begins to open. "It would make more sense if you got off at the floor above."

"You can tell them we have an appointment."

"Why would I want to tell them that?"

"If I go to the tenth floor, will you come with me?"

"That's not what I had in mind. I hope you're not going to force me to do something I don't want to do."

That's the moment it hits me that I'm a character in some collective soap-operatic melodrama, and to the local authorities and whoever else (you of course included), I'm a dangerous person. Since this perception will follow me whatever I do, I see no useful reason to disabuse you of it. "I think you'd better come with me," I say, holding on to your arm until the elevator is in flight again.

An hour later, we are sitting on the third step of the stairwell between the fourteenth and fifteenth floors. You continue to insist that you don't know me, have been aware of my presence only once before when I spoke to you outside of Ernesto's, and that we did not (and do not) have an appointment for any time this afternoon.

"Please don't take this the wrong way," you say. "This is not meant to be disparaging but your behavior suggests that you're more or less delusional. I can assure you that whoever you think I am, I am not that person."

I offer some of the landmarks of our history together, the better times as they seemed to me, in the hope of moving you to some acknowledgment. "I wish I could help you," you say carefully "but I can't. Sorry. May I go now?"

As I see it, no one, not me certainly, least of all me, is keeping you from going wherever you want, but I'm not going to encourage you to leave me by informing you of your rights. "I'd prefer you stayed with me," I say.

Our stalemate continues for awhile (I can't say exactly how much time passes) and then you say, "What if I said that I did know you once, awhile back; if I did say as much, would you let me leave?"

I tend to be prepared for the unexpected—what else is there?—but it's what I dare not hope for that generally takes me by surprise. "Well," I say, "what exactly are you saying?"

"Do we have an agreement?"

"OK," I say, giving nothing away. "Where were we the first time we met? Can you tell me that?"

You cover your face with your hands as if trying to envision something that refuses to come into focus. "In an elevator," you say after some hesitation.

I refuse exhilaration, retain an uneasy calm. Possibly something I said gave you the clue you needed. "An elevator in what building? Where were you going at the time?"

"It was a party in New York City," you say. "I can't remember now whose party but I believe it was in an Upper West Side apartment. Is that your recollection?"

I may have mentioned in a recent conversation that we had a history of meeting in elevators and you filed the information away. "Is this a party trick you're doing for my benefit?"

"If it is, I'm unaware of it. My memory has always been hit or miss and it's gotten worse."

"Did we talk at all at this party?"

"I don't remember," you say. "I don't think we did." You glance at me for confirmation.

My own memories are so variable, so undermined by internal contradictions that I find it hard to distinguish between what's real if any memory is ever real and what's invented for the sake of a more compelling story. Even so, your version of things is too close to my own story to be wholly trusted. In fact, the second time we met there was no indication that you even remembered that there had been a first.

"What happened in San Remy?" I ask.

The question seems to puzzle you. "What's Sand Remy?" you ask.

"If you can tell me what happened in San Remy," I say, "you are free to leave. By the way, it's 'San' not 'sand.'"

You again bury your face in your hands. "San Remy," you say, testing the sound. "Could you give me some clues, some context?"

"No clues," I say.

Several minutes pass or possibly hours, the waiting becoming increasingly burdensome. At some point, I decide to offer you the missing context. "It was at a wedding in Paris that we ran into each other after a long period of separation. I was there alone. You were there with some French guy, I believe. Somehow you had gotten your hands on the key to some cabin in San Remy—you may not have known the name of the town at the time—and after your boyfriend walked out, you invited me to go with you in his place. Do you remember any of this?"

"I ran into you at a wedding in France, is that right, at which my boyfriend and I broke up? And then, after the proceedings, we went together to this town you mention in the south of France."

"And what happened between us during the two months or so we stayed together in the cabin outside San Remy?"

"I don't know really. There are some images in my head, but I can't make much sense of them."

"Describe the images."

You turn away, a sly smile on your face. "Did you bully me like this in San Remy?"

On three separate occasions, there is some vaguely threatening activity just outside the stairwell and I expect each time that you will call for help but you make a point of being absolutely silent.

"On the contrary. When we began to get on each other's nerves, you complained that I was too nice."

You take me in, your eyes narrowed for just that purpose. "Whatever I might have meant by that," you say. "It could be that you were trying too hard. Or that there was something about you or something about my feelings toward you that I found disturbing. This is total conjecture, you understand."

"And what might you have done in such a situation, feeling as you did?"

"What would I have done? What do you mean by that? I don't know what you mean. This is all theoretical, isn't that right? ... I would have, I don't know, tried to get rid of you."

"Get rid of me?"

"I'm impulsive. When I feel oppressed, I strike out. I would have, I don't know, tried to get you out of my hair. I don't remember any of this."

"What would you have done to get rid of me?"

"I don't remember any of this. It might have been you after all who left me. Or maybe I discovered that you were planning to leave. It's painful to be left. And being excessively nice while being repellingly oppressive is a basic form of passive-aggressive hostility. At the very least, it asks for mistreatment in return. My feelings have always confused me as if they were in some language that seemed familiar but were in the most important ways untranslatable. I wanted you out of my life."

"And?"

"It was you who ran away from me. Perhaps I did something that provoked you to leave."

I get up from the step, my back stiff from the awkwardness of the position. "You're free to go," I say. "I'm satisfied."

You continue to sit scrunched down on your step. "Are you sure?"

"This is the way it ends," I say.

"With my going?"

"Yes."

"And what if, for the sake of argument, I refuse to go? What if I decided to stay here with you or go back to New York with you and resume whatever it is we left unfinished? What if I said I loved you? Does that change everything?"

"What are you proposing?"

"Nothing real," you say. "This is all conjecture."

"This is all conjecture" is the last line of my novel. Now you are free to close the book and put it down on the end table next to your bed or slip it into the bookcase in the appropriate alphabetical spot. Even so, I'd be pleased, grateful really, if you held on to it a moment longer so even as we separate, the book, which is my other self, remains close to you, its final page unturned.

Born in Brooklyn, Jonathan Baumbach, the son of a painter and father of a filmmaker, is the author of sixteen much-heralded books, including the much-heralded *B, On the Way to My Father's Funeral, D-Tours, Separate Hours, Reruns, Babble, The Life and Times of Major Fiction, A Man to Conjure With,* and *Dreams of Molly.* His short stories have been widely anthologized, including *O.Henry Prize Stories, All Our Secrets are the Same,* and *Best American Short Stories.* He has written extensively on film and is a former chairman of the National Society of Film Critics. In 1973, Baumbach co-founded (with Peter Spielberg) Fiction Collection, the first national fiction writers cooperative in America (later reinvented as FC2). He has had cameo roles in all of his son Noah's films.